Paula
The Waldensian

**Cover Art:
James Converse**

PAULA
The Waldensian

by
Eva Lecomte

Adapted and translated from the Spanish Version
by
W. M. Strong

A. B. PUBLISHING, INC.
www.abpub.com

Ithaca, Michigan

Preface

I HOPE and trust that the young people who read this book will have as much joy in the reading of it as I have had in its writing.

Paula's Saviour wishes to be your Saviour too. Paula was by no means perfect, but she did love God with all her heart and her neighbor as herself.

This simple country girl, young and strong, yet so tender-hearted and forgetful of self, appears to me sometimes like one of the clear brooks of my beloved land, pure and fresh, slipping noiselessly between flowered banks of forget-me-nots. It was by love that she "conquered"—as we shall see!

If some day you should come to my country, do not forget that I would have great joy in seeing any of those who have read this book. I live in the little town of Villar at the bottom of the valley, where on every side there are hills and mountains as far as the eye can reach. To me it is the loveliest country in the world and I am sure that Paula thought so too.

And so good-bye, dear young reader! I must not keep you any longer, for I am sure you have a great desire to know about Paula; and anyway, I suppose you will have done what I would have done at your age, namely, read the story first, and left my poor preface to the last—for which I have already pardoned you!

And now, may God bless you, Paula dear, as you walk among these my friends who read about you! My prayer is that you may shed over them the same sweet ray of celestial light that you have already shed over others.

Villar-Pelice, France   EVA LECOMTE.

(Translator's note)

"Paula" was originally written in French and translated from thence into Spanish; and the present translator having discovered this literary and spiritual jewel, felt that it should be given also to the young people of the English-speaking world, not only that they might know Paula herself, but that, through her, they might become more intimately acquainted with Paula's Saviour and accept Him as their own Redeemer and Lord.

W. M. STRONG

Coihueco, Chile, South America, 1940.

CONTENTS

PART ONE

PART TWO

PART ONE

Chapter One

AN UNEXPECTED LETTER

Clearly engraved on the walls of my memory there still remains a picture of the great gray house where I spent my childhood. It was originally used for more than a hundred years as the convent of the "White Ladies," with its four long galleries, one above the other, looking proudly down upon the humbler dwellings of the village. On the side of the house, where ran the broad road from the Rouen to Darnetal, a high rugged wall surrounded a wide yard, guarded at the entrance by two massive doors, studded with spikes. The naked barrenness of this yard was, to say the least, forbidding in the extreme; but the fertile fields on the other side of the house spread themselves like a vast and beautiful green carpet, dotted here and there with little villages, crowned with church spires and their corresponding belfries, from which on a Sunday morning pealed out the cheerful call to prayer and worship. The ancient convent long before our story begins had been transformed into a lovely dwelling with an immense garden on one side, edged by a dozen little brick houses that seemed so small that they made us children think of certain doll-houses that we used to see in the Paris magazines. They were known locally as the "Red Cottages." A long avenue of ancient elms separated us from these houses of our neighbors, and in front of the cottages stretched a line of stone benches, where, in the shade of the great trees, the old men of the village used to sit and recount to us tales of the days when the

Convent flourished. Some of these stories made us shiver. (Indeed, they had a habit of straying into our dreams at night.) The rest of the land around the Convent had, with the passing of the years, fallen into the hands of the villagers themselves. Each one had a small space for flowers in the front and a vegetable garden behind.

Of course, our own garden covering the whole space in front of the Red Cottages, was a much more pretentious affair with its deep well, its many-colored kiosks, and its noisy bee-hives. In fact, it was in our eyes, the most enchanting corner of the earth.

I don't remember all the details about the special thing that happened one day, but I know that I shall never forget it to the end of my life.

We were at tea in the garden. Teresa, our old servant, was walking up and down in her kitchen. She never seemed to have time to sit down to eat. Dear old Teresa! She always seemed like a mother to me, for we had lost our own dear mother when I was still in the cradle.

My brother and I had quarreled over a mere nothing, when we were called in to tea by our father. Of course, we did not dare continue our dispute openly in front of him, but we continued our war-like activities by kicking each other under the table.

Louis was ten years old and I was nine. As he was older and a boy, he of course, considered that he had the right to the last word. Now kicks had replaced words; but as we were seated at quite a distance from one another, we did not succeed in causing very much damage to each other's shins. Notwithstanding this, I began to lose patience, and in order to end the matter, knowing that Louis was not very courageous, I leaned my chair as far inside as I could and let him have one terrific kick. At this, his face changed color and my father now disturbed by the extra noise of my kick, finally began to realize what was happening. I do not know how matters would have terminated, if Teresa had not at this moment come into the garden with a black-bordered letter in her hand which she delivered to our father. He took it silently and opened it as Teresa carried away the tea-pot.

I saw immediately by my father's expression that the letter carried serious news, and I am sure Louis noticed it also for he completely forgot to return my kick.

"Teresa!" called my father.

"All right, I'm coming," said the good lady.

"Read this, and tell me what you think of it," and my father handed the letter to the old servant.

Teresa seated herself at the end of the table between Louis and me, and with her head in her hand commenced to read— Teresa was not very well-educated and she read the letter very slowly and half-aloud. "Who wrote this?" was her first question.

"The Pastor of the village," replied my father.

"A minister!" exclaimed Teresa. "He's a mighty poor writer for a minister, and no doubt his mother paid mighty well for his 'education'."

My father smiled a bit sadly.

"You don't understand it, Teresa?"

"Yes, yes; I understand half of it, and I think I can guess the other half."

"Do you want me to help you?" offered Louis.

Teresa looked scornfully at Louis—

"You! I should say not! You don't care to help me in the kitchen or run errands for me, and the only thing the matter with you now is curiosity!"

That settled Louis, and Teresa went on with her reading. Bending her great fat form more and more closely over the letter, she became more serious as she neared the bottom of the fourth page where the writing became so close and so fine that it was hardly possible to decipher it. When, at last, she lifted her head, her eyes were full of tears. "Poor, poor little thing!" she repeated softly.

"Well, what do you think?" said my father.

"What do I think? Why we must send at once and have her come here as soon as possible, because—"

"Who?" my father interrupted her without ceremony.

"Yes; who? who?" questioned Louis.

"Tell us, father, please," added my sister Rosa, a tall serious girl of fifteen.

And as he did not answer us quickly our questions multiplied.

"Patience! Patience!" cried my father; "your turn will come."

"Teresa, you are getting old, and another girl in the house simply means more work for you and a lot more problems for me. If 'she' (my father had never been able to reconcile himself to pronounce the name of my mother since her untimely death)—if 'she' were here I would not hesitate, but to bring another orphan into a family already half-orphaned doesn't seem right to me."

"Don't worry, sir, a little more work doesn't worry Teresa Rouland. She will have to get up a little earlier and go to bed a little later, and that will be all."

"Well, Teresa, I'll think about it, and it needs to be 'thought about' a good deal."

"And why do you say that, sir? One doesn't have to reflect long about doing good."

"Well, I'll tell you why I hesitate. I'm sure that someone else could much better replace the parents of this orphaned girl. I must confess that for my part I don't feel equal to the task."

"Sir, would you like to know what I think? You have said to yourself, 'From the time that my wife died life has become a burden, and if it wasn't for the children I would have died of grief, but for love of them I must work and live. Therefore, with my heart torn and desolated as it is, I don't feel called upon to take any responsibility upon myself other than that of my own children!'"

"There is a good deal of truth in what you say, Teresa."

"Yes, sir, but it is very bad, very bad, if you will let me say so! I know I ought not to talk so, as I'm only a poor old servant; but remember, I was the one that brought up the lovely woman that we all mourn for, and I knew her before you did, sir, and I loved her as if she were my own child. When I put her in the coffin it was as if they had taken out a piece of my own heart. She was so young to die, so sweet, so good, and besides so marvelously beautiful! But I dried my tears as best I could, for I knew there was much to be done; and I said to myself that I would honor the memory of my mistress by doing always that which I knew she would have approved of. And now, sir, take this little orphan as you know your good wife would have done, as the daughter of her beloved sister..." She stopped suddenly, slightly abashed, as she realized that perhaps she had said a little too much for one in her station in life.

But more than her mere words, her voice vibrant with emotion had moved us all to the depths of our souls.

"You are a valiant woman with a great heart," my father said, as he took her hand. "I will write this very night and ask them to send the girl to us as soon as possible."

Then turning to us he added, "You no doubt know by this time of whom we have been speaking. Your cousin Paula has just lost her father. You will remember, her mother died some years ago, and we are her nearest relatives. You uncle's friends have written me as to whether I will consent to receive Paula in our home, and in a few days, more or less, she will be among us."

We opened our mouths to ask a thousand questions, but father stopped us. "No, no! That is enough for now! Later I will tell you the details; besides, I must go out immediately. Go now to your various tasks and don't be thinking too much about this coming of your cousin."

Chapter Two

MEMORIES

That night I could not study my lessons. In fact, I could do nothing but think about Paula! I was not a student and was always at the bottom of the class. Louis, in the matter of study, was no better than I; but in the school, thanks to his brilliancy of mind, he always seemed to skin through somehow. Rosa was not a bit like her brother and sister; being a model of patience, application and obedience. I was very proud of my sister Rosa, and I loved and admired her, but I never had the slightest desire to imitate her.

After my father had gone, nothing was talked of except our cousin Paula. When would she come? What would she be like? Would she be content to be here among us? All these were questions which we could not answer as we knew very little about her. They had told me that Paula lived in the Waldensian Valley—a country where the inhabitants fed on black bread and lived in homes that were like stables. I had no idea just exactly where the mountains of Piedmont were. I had searched the map without being able to find the region, but I supposed it must be somewhere between France, Italy and Switzerland.

There was another thing I had found out; namely, that Paula was about my own age. What happiness! This fact I repeated over and over until Louis told me to keep quiet. This attitude on his part I put down as discontent because Paula wasn't a boy, so I kept repeating, "Paula's the same as me!"

"For mercy's sake, will you keep quiet, Lisita? Besides you have your grammar twisted as usual. It doesn't surprise me in the least that you're always at the foot of the class, if that's the way you study."

"You can talk to me as you like," I answered, "but when Paula gets here I'll never speak to you again, and I'll tell her not to say a word to you either. I am mighty glad that Paula's a girl and not a disagreeable boy like you."

"Oh, keep your Paula, much do I care!" replied Louis.

"Come, come," exclaimed Rosa, "what's the good of fighting over this poor girl Paula whom neither of you have ever seen!"

"It's Louis' fault!"

"No, it's Lisita's!"

"It's the two of you! If Paula could see the way you quarrel I'm sure she would not want to come. I hope she will love us all and we must all of us love her also, because she's not only an orphan, but she's a niece of our poor dear, dead mother."

Rosa knew well how to bring about peace. One word about our mother was enough.

"See here, Lisita," and Rosa drew me toward her, "I see that you haven't the slightest desire to study tonight, so close your book, and if you get up early tomorrow morning I'll help you. Do you know what I would do now if I were you."

"What?"

"I'd go and see Catalina. You know that she does not like to be alone all of the afternoon, and I think Teresa has gone out. If I didn't have so much to do I'd see her myself. Now, look out you don't make too much noise. Catalina has a terrible headache today."

"All right. I'm off!" I said.

The idea of visiting my oldest sister never made me very happy in those days. In fact, I hardly ever entered her room because it bored me terribly to be in the company of such a disagreeable invalid.

I remembered the time when Catalina was the liveliest and happiest person in the whole house, but unfortunately all this had changed in an instant. One day three years before, Catalina had fallen from the top of a high cherry-tree which she had climbed against the advice of Teresa. She was unconscious when we picked her up, and it seemed at first as if she would die as a result of the fall. After six months of cruel suffering, however, her youth had triumphed over death; but the big sister who had always been as happy and as lively as a bird was gone from us, and in her place remained a forlorn, unhappy girl with a poor twisted body, who at rare intervals sallied from her room a few steps with the aid of her crutches. Unfortunately her character had also suffered severely, for in spite of the tenderness and solicitude of my father who sought to satisfy her slightest desire, and in spite of the untiring care of Teresa and the patience and sweetness of Rosa, Catalina's life was one long complaint. Her room, with its white bed adorned with blue curtains and its magnificent view of the fields and mountains, was the most beautiful in the whole house. A pair of canaries sang for her in their respective corners; the finest fruits were always for her; and as she was a great reader, new books were continually brought in; but nothing seemed to have power to put a smile of satisfaction on her thin, wasted face.

Poor Catalina! It was certainly true—I didn't love her very much. I was so accustomed to see my sister in her invalid state that her pitiful condition didn't seem to move me, and she was always in such a bad humor that I only went to see her on rare occasions.

However, on this particular afternoon, I had, of course, a great desire to carry her the news of our cousin's coming, and so I gladly went to visit her; but forgetting all the warnings of Rosa I burst open the door like a gust of wind.

Catalina was lying with her face toward the wall with the curtains of the bed partly drawn, and a green shade had been placed over the cages of the two birds in order to stop their singing. Under other circumstances I would have prudently retired, thinking that Catalina, more irritated or sicker than usual, was endeavoring to sleep. Doubtless our old servant had come in to speak to her regarding Paula, and finding her apparently asleep had arranged things as I found them. She turned her head on hearing me come in and in a sharp tone exclaimed, "What a noise, Lisita! Can't you give me a single quiet moment!"

"You know I haven't been here all day!" I answered impatiently. "In fact, I haven't been here since yesterday morning, and besides, I forgot that Rosa told me that you had a headache."

"Well, you know it now!"

"So you wouldn't care to have me tell you the big news!"

"No!"

"Well, I am going to tell you anyhow, because I can't keep it to myself any longer! Uncle John is dead!"

"Uncle John! Dead?"

"Yes, and I'm happy!"

"What do you mean, you're happy!"

"Well, I am happy!--not because Uncle John is dead but because his little girl, Paula, who is just my age, is coming to live with us, so, of course, why shouldn't I be happy?"

"Well, you can just forget your 'happiness,' because Paula is *not* going to live with us. I can tell you that right now!"

"And why not? Father said she was coming! You can ask Teresa, or Rosa, or Louis!"

"I am not going to ask anyone, but I tell you that Paula is *not* coming here! NO! And indeed, NO! I've got enough to put up with, with Louis and you! It seems as if you tear my head apart, for you quarrel from morning till night; and when you play it seems as if the house is coming down; and now suppose another bad-mannered little girl should come among us! But I tell you it *never* shall happen!"

"You're not the one who orders things here!"

"Neither do you, you impertinent little thing."

"Now, don't get mad, Catalina!" I cried, as I burst into tears.

"You don't know what you are talking about. You do not realize that Paula has no one in the world to care for her. Teresa read us the letter out loud. I know I'm not a good girl and I'm almost as disagreeable as you are, but I am going to be good when Paula comes. You shall see. She will be my dearly beloved sister and she is almost exactly my age. Oh, I certainly shall love her so, and we shall always be together and we, we..."

"Keep quiet, Lisita. You tongue runs like a mill-wheel. Besides, where did you get all these details?"

"It was this afternoon, just as we finished tea. They wrote to father, and father gave the letter to Teresa, and Teresa said that a little extra work didn't bother her, and so father said, 'All right, let her come!'"

"And I? Father said nothing about me?"

"Not that I remember."

"Oh," sobbed Catalina, "everything is done without me now! Because I am nothing more than an invalid, everything is arranged without consulting me! What difference does it make to you—who are able to laugh and run and play—if I suffer here without having a thing to say about what goes on in the house! How would you like to be in my place? Father never came to say one single word to me about the matter, and now without consulting me as to whether it would disturb me, they wish to bring another trouble to torment me more! But it shall not be, and the day that she comes I shall go to a hospital, because they do not want me here any more!"

Poor Catalina! She had passed a very bad day, and always on such days she would weep on the slightest pretext. I didn't care for her very much, but that day I pitied her with all my heart, and I did what I could to calm her; for once her nerves were excited, nothing could console the poor unhappy girl. Besides, I was very much afraid that she would be able to change my father's purpose in regard to Paula. He, generally so severe, so cold and insensible in his attitude toward us, obeyed the slightest wish of his eldest daughter. And if—if— she succeeded in preventing Paula's coming I felt that I would never, never pardon Catalina! But now I tried to embrace her.

"Listen," I said; "father had to go out, but when he returns he will tell you the same thing that I have told you!"

But Catalina would not hear me. With her head hidden in the pillows, she continued crying.

I was desperate! As a rule it took a lot less than this to make Catalina worse. Catalina worse! And all my fault! What would my father say! And yet I had had no bad intentions. How could I have known that she would have received my good news this way? Suddenly I had a brilliant idea. Leaving Catalina I ran to the kitchen where Teresa was preparing the vegetables for supper. "Teresa , come quickly," I cried with my eyes full of tears; "Catalina is making herself sick with crying."

"And why? I left her sleeping only a short time ago."

"Oh yes, I know; but please come at once, Teresa! It's all my fault! I told her that Paula was coming and she is beside herself! But really and truly I had no idea she would take it that way!"

Teresa jumped up quickly, saying under her breath, "What next?" and then to me, "You certainly are a troublesome youngster, my poor Lisita!"

"But Teresa, I vow to you . . ."

"Be quiet, and go back to Catalina's room! I'll be there as soon as I can!"

I left the kitchen well content. Teresa was not full of pretty phrases but she had a heart of gold, and I knew somehow or other she would be able to fix things with Catalina. I found Rosa already in Catalina's room on my return, trying in vain to calm her. She turned to me.

"What on earth has happened? I heard Catalina sobbing, clear at the other end of the house. Are you responsible for this?"

"No, no, it wasn't I: it was Paula."

"Paula!"

I tried to explain, but at this minute Teresa entered, bringing with her a plateful of delicious apples.

"Come, come, Catalina!" and her deep, sonorous voice seemed like soothing balm, as her presence appeared to fill the room. "What on earth are you crying about? It is but a short moment ago that I secured permission from your papa to read you a letter which he has just received from Italy, and I went out to pick up some of your favorite apples, the first of the season, and here I come to find you crying!"

Catalina became a little calmer hearing the word "letter," for, to the poor confined invalid, a letter from abroad was a great event. Nevertheless, between her sobs she remarked, "Is it a letter about this terrible 'Paula' that they are talking about?"

"Yes," answered Teresa, with that soothing voice of hers. "It's a letter that tells us a bit about a niece of your poor mother."

Catalina calmed down completely. If the memory of our mother still lived in the heart of her other daughters it had first place above all else with Catalina.

"Now, read it to me, Catalina," said Teresa. "You can do so much better than I can in the reading line, and it will sound so much better from your lips than from my poor stumbling ones. Wait till I fix up the pillows, and don't cry any more. And now your headache is better, isn't it?"

"It still pains terribly, Teresa. Let Rosa read it."

Rosa took the letter, and read in her clear, sweet voice the lines that had so stirred us all.

There were but a few details. Our Uncle John had died; so wrote the pastor of the little church in that far-off Waldensian Valley. He had died as he had lived—a real Christian. He had no near relatives, it appeared; and the rest of the family had gone to America two years before. Paula, therefore, was alone. Just before breathing his last, my uncle had expressed the desire to leave his daughter in the care of our father whom he had never known, but of whom he had heard nothing but good. Beside all this he had left his daughter in the hands of God, the loving Father of all orphans, praying Him to guide and direct in the whole affair. His last prayer had been for us; asking God to bless our family that we might all be guided into the straight and narrow Way that leadeth unto life eternal. Then followed certain details relative to a small inheritance that Paula possessed, and the prayer of the Pastor himself that the temporal and spiritual happiness of the little orphan might be maintained.

"Is that all?" asked Catalina.

"Yes," said Rosa; "that is the end of the letter."

"Poor little thing!"

There was a long silence. I think Catalina was thinking of her mother, for her face had softened for once.

Teresa sat with her large agile fingers flying,—those strong fingers that were never idle;—the metallic sound of her needles alternating with the happy song of the canaries, from whose cages the curtains had again been removed.

Never in my life had I lingered very long to observe Catalina, but this afternoon I could not help but notice how pale and delicate she really was. Propped up on her pillows with her golden hair falling around her shoulders, one would not have guessed her to be more than fourteen years old, instead of eighteen. Seeing her thus after her day of sufferings, I pardoned all her bad humor and hardness of heart toward Paula; and I had a great desire to take her in my arms but I did not dare do such a thing,—fearing she would refuse my caresses.

"Teresa," she said suddenly, closing her eyes to keep back the tears, "do you think that it hurts very much when one dies?"

"Why do you ask that?" and Teresa looked at her quite surprised.

"I was thinking of Uncle John."

"That depends, Catalina, that depends. There are some persons who die tranquilly in their sleep with no pain at all, but in the case of others it is quite the contrary."

"But afterward, Teresa! How about afterward? What happens to us after death?"

"Afterward?" Teresa looked puzzled. "Nobody knows what happens to us afterward. When I was a little girl, my mother who was a very pious woman, told us that if we were very good we would go to heaven, but if we were bad we went to hell. I believe she was right, poor woman, but it is sometime since I have thought of religious things, and your father does not like to have us talk about it."

"I know that, Teresa, but I can't help thinking about it often and often. Was our mother a 'pious woman?'"

"Not exactly—at least, not before she became ill. Her relatives in Villar—your Aunt and your uncle John used to write lovely letters to her that spoke of God and heaven and prayer. Your mother used to sigh after reading them, and sometimes she would read me a page or two from those letters, and would say to me, 'My good Teresa, we both ought to think about these things! My sister is far more happy in her hut on the mountain-side in Waldensia than we are here in the midst of abundance. It must be wonderful not to fear death and to love God with all our heart.' When she spoke thus to your father he laughed at her and said, 'Now don't you worry about that, darling, you couldn't be any better than you are now; and I am glad that you are not like these pious ladies who try to tell you what will happen to you after death. You'll have plenty of time to think about those things when you come to your last days; but now with your good health and robust constitution you can count on a good old age.'"

"But father was mistaken, Teresa!"

"Yes, he certainly was mistaken, poor man. Nobody could have believed that when on that Monday afternoon she complained of a little pain in her throat, she would die on the following Thursday."

"Was it diphtheria, Teresa?"

All that poor Teresa could say amid her tears was, "Poor, poor little beloved one! Never shall I forget her last moments or the desperation of your father. From his very first visit the doctor said that there was no hope. I thought I would go insane when he said that! How I remember her the day before she was taken ill, in all her youth and beauty—singing as she worked, and then suddenly came that terrible pressure in her throat."

"Then, Teresa, you remember, she could not kiss us goodbye."

"No, poor lady, that was her greatest pain when they told her that her sickness was very contagious. But—there! there! Catalina, I did not mean to make you cry, and I have told you this story so many times, and now here I am telling it over again like the foolish woman I am!"

"No, no, Teresa, go on," answered Catalina between her sobs. "I am always happy when I hear you speak of our beloved Mamma."

And now, I too could not keep back my tears as I kneeled beside the old servant, who left her work to pass her hand over my head.

"Thou didst not know her, dear Lisita. How many times during her sickness she told me especially to take care of thee, and love thee as if I were thine own mother. Yes, and correct thee also . . . At times I ask myself whether I have obeyed her."

"Oh, Teresa," exclaimed Rosa, interrupting her and closing, with a bang the book which she had not read. "Indeed, you have done your duty. What would we have done without you? Of course, I can't say," and Rosa smiled, "that your punishments have been very numerous, but father has taken care of that. Father corrects us and you do the loving part."

"Now, see here, your father loves you also, and it's only the pain of having lost your mother that makes him appear more severe than he really is. Open the window Rosa, I can hardly see, and I must finish this stocking before I quit tonight."

Rosa obeyed, and a soft breeze entered, laden with the perfume of the garden, and Teresa resumed; "After the doctor had gone that afternoon your mother called me and said, 'Teresa tell me the truth. The doctor believes I am going to die; does he not?' I didn't know what to answer her. Your father hoped in spite of the doctor's opinion that she'd pull through, and did not wish me to let your poor mother know that there was any danger. But here she lay praying me with her joined hands that I should tell her the truth. She spoke with great difficulty and I feared that soon she would not be able to speak at all, and therefore weeping, told her the whole truth.

"And then?"

"Then she said to me, 'Teresa, I'm certainly afraid to die! I'm afraid! I'm afraid!'

" 'But,' said I, 'Madame, why should you be afraid? You have always been so good to everybody. The good God will take you to heaven.' But she could not be calm.

"'According to the world's standard perhaps yes, Teresa— but before God! To think that soon I shall be face to face with the Lord Jesus and am not prepared! No, no, let me speak, Teresa! I have done my duty to my husband and by my children, but I have forgotten God. I have not loved Him, neither have I prayed to Him and therefore I'm afraid to meet Him. Oh, Teresa, I'm afraid to die.'

"I could only repeat, 'The good God will pardon you, Madame. He is so good and kind. He will have pity on you, for you have never done any harm to anybody.'

" 'Ah,' she answered, 'if I had but listened to my sister and brother-in-law! How many times they urged me in their letters to surrender to the Lord Jesus, but I always put it off...and now I'm dying! Oh, Teresa, Teresa, can you not help me?'"

"But I thought Mamma died in peace?" suddenly questioned Rosa. "I remember toward the end that she was anxious to go, and at last said that she was going to heaven."

"Yes, my beloved madame did indeed die in peace. Sometime after she had asked me whether I could help her she said, 'Teresa, read again the last letter from my sister. I have it here under my pillow.' I read it to her as best I could, and as I finished she said to me, 'Read it again, Teresa. Oh, if only my dead sister were here this minute!" Twice again I read the letter, but still she was not satisfied. 'Those last words, Teresa. Read them again to me, please.' And again I read them."

"Do you remember those last words, Teresa?" Catalina asked as she listened with rapt attention to the story she had heard so often from the lips of our old servant.

"I don't remember all. I would have liked to have kept the letter. It was such a letter that would help anyone to die, for it was certainly a treasure. But my poor madame wished to carry it to the tomb with her, and no doubt it is there yet in her hands, poor little angel. As I remember it, the letter concluded thus: 'He that believeth on Me hath everlasting life, and him that cometh to Me I will in no wise cast out!'"

"I read these, the last words of the letter, a dozen times over to her and she seemed to take hold of them as a drowning man would grasp a board that floated by him—then without movement, with her eyes shut, she seemed to be sleeping, but every once in a while she appeared to be talking with someone."

"Do you think she was praying, Teresa?" I asked in a trembling voice.

"Yes, Lisita, she was praying. And I am sure that the good God heard her, for she said to me after a long silence, 'Teresa, I believe my Saviour has taken me for His own—I am a poor, guilty, and ungrateful sinner—I have waited until the last moment, and I know my sins are great, but my

Saviour's love is greater. But oh, my husband! And my children! I have done nothing to attract them to God. Oh, Teresa, take care of them! Take care of them! I have put them in the hands of the Lord that He may save them also. I can do nothing and—it is too late!'

"She asked me to call your father who was resting in the next room for he had watched all the previous night and had worked as usual all day. She could hardly speak, but as best she could, she prayed him to be reconciled to God and to teach their children to know the way of salvation."

"The strange thing to me, Teresa," said Rosa thoughtfully, "is that our father who loved our mother so much, has not taught us this Christian religion according to our dear mother's last wish."

"That is the terrible part," Teresa answered. "An awful change came on him at the death of your mother. He loved her desperately and when she died it seemed as if his heart turned to stone, and when I tried to console him he cried out bitterly, 'Don't speak to me of God and don't try to tell me He is a God of love. He took away my most precious treasure and tore my heart and my very life to pieces.'

"About a week after the death of my poor madame he called me to him and said, 'Teresa, you are a good woman. You've brought up my dear Maria, carried her in your arms when she was small, and in your arms she drew her last breath. She commended her poor children into your hands, and I want you to remain forever at their side, but on one condition, remember—that you never speak to them again on the subject of religion, neither of prayer, nor of church, nor anything of the kind. Hear me well, Teresa! Hear me! I have prayed very little in my life, but on that last night when my dear wife passed away, if anyone prayed with all his heart and all his strength, I did so. Kneeling beside her bed I promised God to serve Him; to bring up my children for Him if He would only leave me my treasure. But He didn't do it. Then why should I serve Him?'

"When I saw that it was useless to argue with him I promised what he asked. Just think, if I had been obliged to abandon you to a strange servant!" and Teresa viewed the three of us with those great blue eyes of hers full of affection for us.

"Oh," I cried, trying to take her great fat body in my arms, "What would we have done without you!"

But Teresa, wanting very much to cry and yet trying hard not to show it, put me gently aside, saying, "There, there! You are making me lose a lot of time. Stand up, stand up! You have been on the floor at my feet for over half-an-hour like a little purring kitten and wearing out your stockings besides."

And then continuing without awaiting my reply:

"Well, I am only a poor ignorant servant. If I can read, it is because my poor madame taught me. Nevertheless it has nearly broken my heart to see all three of you, and Louis besides, growing up like a bunch of heathen. And, what happiness prayer does bring one!"

"Do you pray, Teresa?" asked the wondering Rosa.

"Oh, at times. But see now, servants must do what they see their masters do. After the death of my poor madame, I prayed often, but little by little I seemed to lose the habit. Your father hardly ever spoke to me, and excepting Catalina, you were all too small to understand important things, and the neighbors! Oh, you know among our neighbors one never hears any prayers at their houses either. I would be so happy before I die to see the day when my poor madame's prayers be heard regarding us."

"It's a shame," said Rosa, "that Paula is so small. If she were only a few years older perhaps she could"—"I'll tell you what's a shame, and that is that she coming at all," interrupted Catalina with the return of her bad humor.

"Oh," sighed Teresa, "poor little thing! What could she do at her age! A child of ten years will never be able to change your father's ideas. The more you speak to him the worse he is. No, the one who has to change will be the child *herself!* She must learn to do as we do. I do hope she may not have to suffer too much. Of course, at her age she will adapt herself quickly to her surroundings, and after all, your father is a good-hearted man. There! At last the sock is done! It was time, for I cannot see any more. What a lovely day it has been! The fruit ought to ripen quickly with a few more days like this."

One, two, three, four, five, six, seven, eight, nine . . . it was the great clock of Darnetal that recalled us to the present.

"Nine o'clock!" exclaimed Teresa, "how the time has passed! Lisita! Off to bed!"

"Please, Teresa, let me stay a few minutes more; it's lovely here by the open window."

"Yes, it won't be so lovely tomorrow morning when you must rise early to be in class on time. Isn't that so? Now go, Lisita! No more nonsense!"

"Here, take this," said Catalina, handing me a lovely orange that she had received; "you can have it if you go to bed immediately!"

"Oh," I exclaimed beamingly; "I do love you so, dear Catalina."

"Is it me or the orange you love?"

"It's you, and the orange, and Teresa, and Papa, and Rosa, and Louis, and Paula."

"There! there! Go to bed," said Catalina, disentangling herself from my arms. "If you don't go to bed at once I will take away your orange."

Laughing, I embraced her again, and Rosa too, and then rushed off to my room, but not without slamming Catalina's door with a noise that shook the whole house.

Chapter Three

PAULA ARRIVES

For nearly a week I couldn't think of another thing but the coming of Paula. My father had gone to Paris. He would be there some days to arrange certain important matters of business in connection with his factory, and also to wait for the little orphan to be placed in his care by a lady who was journeying from Villar to Paris. In school I talked of nothing else. In fact, I talked about her all day and every day. I learned nothing, nor could I seem to do anything around the house.

One night, while dreaming, I jumped from the bed, crying, "Paula! Paula!" This awakened Teresa, and she made me take some nasty medicine thinking I had fever. I made promises of reform. I wanted to be good, studious and patient, in order to be an example to Paula who would see my good qualities and would thus endeavor to imitate me. Nevertheless I became absolutely insufferable! My older sisters without being quite so enthusiastic as I was, nevertheless spoke often of Paula. Catalina began to worry that Paula might suffer in our house, but she soon consoled herself by remembering that my father had promised to put her out to board, if it turned out that she could not get along amicably with us. As to Louis, he soon showed us that he was not at all interested in the arrival of his young cousin. If it had been a boy, it would have been different—but a girl!

Teresa spoke very little as to Paula, but I am persuaded that long before the arrival of our little orphan cousin, she had been given a large place in our old servant's heart. She found a little white bed up in the attic, which was placed in my room beside my own cot.

At last the great day arrived. It was a Wednesday, and of course I had to go to school as usual. We did not know at what hour my father would come from Paris with Paula, and so, every moment I said to myself, "Perhaps they have arrived!" Result—my lessons went from bad to worse, but at last at five in the afternoon, I reached the house breathless only to find that Paula had not yet come. "They are not coming!" I cried impatiently, "I knew they wouldn't be here!"

"Then why did you run so fast?" Teresa asked.

I said nothing, but soon Rosa also arrived, and after tea I put all my books in order, redressed my dolls, got rid of the ink on my hands with pumice-stone, and in between each task, took a walk in the garden on the passing of any coach—but always with the same result! Would they *ever* arrive? Then came supper-time. Catalina had been up and dressed all day and would not hear of going to bed until Paula came. Our summer days are very long, but night had arrived, the lamps had been lighted, and we had resigned ourselves to wait without the consolation of seeing the road from the window. Then suddenly—Oh, joy! We heard a faint sound of wheels in the distance; then clearer and clearer as they rattled over the pavement of the deserted street. Teresa had already arisen from her chair. I had a wild desire to run out in the dark to receive my young cousin for whom I had waited all these weeks, but something seemed to detain me. Then while I waited questioning myself as to what I would say to Paula, trying to remember all the many counsels of Teresa, our old servant staggered in from the yard with a great bag in each hand. Then our father entered with a young girl at his side dressed in black. Paula had come!

In anticipation I had fancied Paula as a pale, sad little girl with blue eyes full of tears. She would have golden hair, very smooth, cut off at the base of her ears, and would be dressed in black muslin, and wear a straw hat with a black ribbon tied under her chin. But here was a different Paula. She was large for her age and appeared quite strong. Her frank open face, bronzed with the sun and air, showed health and intelligence. A black silk cap with a wide ribbon of the same color, failed to entirely hide a magnificent head of brown hair, gathered beneath her cap after the manner of the Waldensians. Her simple dress of black and gray stripes reached almost to her ankles, while an apron of fine cretonne came to her knees. A black shawl whose points passed under her arms and were knotted behind, protected her shoulders, while a pair of great thick shoes completed her attire. In spite of what to our mind was a certain quaint oddness in her dress, it could not hide Paula's beauty. Her forehead was broad and intelligent, her large brown eyes were full of certain sweetness, and a lovely smile played on her half-opened lips.

"Come," said our father in an almost kindly voice for him; "Embrace your young cousin, and give her a hearty welcome."

Rosa came forward, and I timidly did the same; but Paula dropping father's hand, rushed toward Rosa and then to me, kissing us both and laughing and crying at the same time. She seemed to forget her long voyage and her weariness as she repeated to each one of us in her melodious voice, "I know I shall love you all, and my Uncle Charles here. I already love him, and he has told me all your names. Let me see, this is Rosa," and then turning to me, "You are Lisita. Oh, if you only knew how much I love you all!"

"Now go and greet your cousin Catalina," said my father. "She is the sick one," he added softly.

Paula drew near the big chair where the sick girl reclined. Catalina was smiling sadly at the young stranger. "Do you also love me a little?" asked my eldest sister.

With tenderness and infinite care Paula enveloped her in her strong arms. "I already love you with all my heart!" she said, laying her head against Catalina's shoulder.

"Have you ever been sick, Paula?" she questioned her.

"No, but Papa was," she said in a trembling tone.

At this moment Teresa arrived carrying in the final bag. "At last," she said, embracing Paula. "Do you know who I am?" Then, seeing that Paula viewed her a bit strangely, she added, "I am only old Teresa. It was I who brought up your dear mother, and I thought I would have to do the same with you; but it looks to me as if you wouldn't need very much of my care. You are so large and healthy, much bigger than Lisita here, and yet you probably are no older. How old are you, pray?"

"I am ten years old, madame."

"Oh, don't call me 'madame.' Call me Teresa, just as your mother did many years ago."

And Teresa took the lamp and brought it close to Paula. "No, you hardly have any similarity in your face, but your voice is like hers. Now, let me hug you once more, my treasure." And Teresa pressed to her heart the motherless child.

"In my country they say I am like Papa. In fact, I have his portrait in the trunk and I will show it to you."

"Show it to us now!" I shouted.

But Teresa interrupted me. "What a child you are, when poor Paula is so tired! Tomorrow will be time enough."

The meal for the young traveler had been prepared on the end of the great table, where Teresa had placed buttered toast and jam. And soon she sallied from the kitchen with the rest of the food.

"There you are, Paula," Teresa said, drawing her to the table; "Sit down and eat!"

"And the others?" said Paula, looking at us.

"Oh, we ate long ago," said Rosa.

"I think we might eat a little bread and jam to accompany her," I said. Then everybody laughed.

"I think Lisita is right for once," said Teresa, always happy when she was able to give us a bit of pleasure, "and I think Paula will be a little more comfortable that way."

"Now then, Paula, are you not hungry?" asked Teresa with her hand on the lock of the kitchen door.

"Yes, madame, . . . that is—yes, Teresa."

"Begin then! Lisita doesn't need any urging. Do as she does, and I trust you will eat with a good appetite."

Paula looked at us, one after the other, and then looked at Teresa as if she would say something. As Teresa remained, looking on in an astonished manner, Paula got down from her chair and stood in front of her now cooling cup of hot milk. She placed her hands together, closing her eyes and bending her head a little, she said slowly and deliberately in a low voice, "The food which we receive, O Lord, may it be blessed, in the name of the Father, and of the Son, and of the Holy Ghost, Amen!"

Chapter Four

PAULA'S TREASURES

Naturally, on awakening the next morning, after Paula's arrival, it was "Paula, Paula, Paula," that occupied my every thought. I found she was still sleeping. How I did wish to wake her up! But Teresa had cautioned me to let her sleep as long as she wished on account of her journey the day before. So I simply half-opened the curtains of her bed and closed the window to warm up the room.

I had no idea what hour it was. Teresa had the watch under her pillow, and I could never tell the time by the sun, like Louis and Rosa, but I could tell it was very early, for almost every door and window of the red houses across the street, were still closed. Once in a while, I saw a factory hand passing with his lunch under his arm, on his way to work. Among these, I noticed one whom we called the "Breton," a terrific drunkard of whom I was greatly afraid; but, strange to say, this morning he went on his way with a firm, straight step, behaving himself quite like an ordinary person.

The sky was clear and very, very blue, without a single cloud. It had rained the night before, for on all the trees and bushes thousands of water-drops glistened like diamonds in the light of the newly risen sun.

Dozens of little birds were singing their morning songs in the great linden trees on the avenue, and the scent of the flowers from the laborers' little gardens over the way, floated in through the window, and what a multitude they were! Roses, lilies, geraniums, pansies and forget-me-nots. I could not see our own garden from our bedroom window, but I knew that it also would have flowers in profusion, thanks to the faithful Teresa's unceasing care. Here also hung that delight

37

of my life—the swing which my father had placed under the apple-tree one happy day five years ago. Oh, how Paula would love it, and how happy she would be among us! Again I took a peep between the curtains but still she slept. Would she ever wake up? Now I had a chance to observe her more closely. That beautiful face, just a bit serious, buried in the white pillow, on which were signs of moisture, betraying the fact that tears had been mixed with her slumbers.

It was long after we finished breakfast, and our father had gone to his work, that she finally awoke. But now, all her sadness had disappeared, and not a sign of a tear remained. She ate her breakfast with great gusto, not however without again performing that strange custom of putting her hands together, and repeating the prayer which our astonished ears had heard the night before.

Teresa searched among my sister's clothes for something a little more modern with which to clothe our little country visitor. Meanwhile Paula chatted happily to us, telling us quite a little of her life in that far-off Waldensian valley. In the winter she and her father had lived in the stable in the midst of the cows, goats, sheep, rabbits, etc. It was the heat from the bodies of these animals that kept them quite warm; and at the same time saved the price of fuel which would otherwise have been necessary if they had stayed during the day in the dwelling-house. Sometimes, she told us, the poor from the village would come to their stable, bringing their children with them for this same purpose of getting warm without any expenditure of fuel. Then, what happiness and what games they had together, in that little space in the stable between animals!

Oh, yes, she went to the school, she said—the little school whose teacher was her own father who every afternoon gathered the children together in that self-same stable. In the evening, the neighbors would bring each one his own little stool, crowding into every unoccupied space that could be found in the stable; the women spinning, the men reading in turn from the Bible by the light of a tallow candle. Meanwhile the babies were put to sleep in the straw above the sheep-fold, until the time came to disperse for the night.

Paula, being a great girl of ten years old, always tried desperately to keep awake along with the older folks. Toward the close of the evening, her father would say, "Now, my friends, let us meet before the Lord." Then the needles would be put away, the hymn-books would be taken out, and often they would sing far into the night. Then after earnest prayers by several of the neighbors, the long winter meeting would break up.

Of course, Paula preferred the summer, she said, when she ran barefoot through the flower-covered fields or when she accompanied her father as they gathered wheat. Then at other times she had to take her turn caring for the flocks of sheep and goats, and see that the lambs and little kids did not stray too far away. She never tired of watching these happy little creatures with their thousand antics as they jumped over the rocks.

In the summer, how happy she was in those vast green Alpine fields, how magnificent that pure air, and that bluest of all blue skies! And in the autumn! What a beautiful season was that, with the nut-gathering and the bringing in of the apples and the grapes. Then she told us how our Uncle John would take the honey from the hives, that golden honey with its heavenly taste.

As she spoke, Paula with her lovely animated face, appeared to live again in her happy past, quite forgetful that she was now far away from her beloved, sunny land of the

Alps, where that dear father slept the sleep of death on the hillside.

I, of course, had been in the habit of hearing our mother speak of her home in the Alps with nothing but sighs and tears. It astonished me now to hear this young creature so full of life and vigor and happiness speak of her old life in Waldensia. I had been preparing myself to console her and endeavor to make her happy and forget her past life of poverty. But now it was quite the contrary. Here was Paula scattering happiness and love all around her, entertaining us and making us laugh at her wonderful stories.

Teresa came and went from one room to another opening boxes, finding here a dress that Catalina could not wear anymore, there an apron that had grown too short for Rosa, and here again a pair of small shoes that would no doubt fit our country cousin, with a black ribbon or two that had formerly served us in our time of mourning when mamma died. From her bed in the other room, Catalina listened, calling me at times to re-tell some of the conversation which she had missed, and Rosa wrote a letter to Louis to tell him in detail all about Paula's arrival.

Of course, we were all in high good humor, but I believe I was the happiest of all, for I certainly loved this newly-arrived cousin of mine and found her a thousand times finer than I had even imagined.

I said to her once without thinking, "Paula, were you very sorry when you lost your father?" Teresa looked at me threateningly, but it was too late! Paula had already heard me and her eyes filled with tears. I would have given a good deal if I could have recalled my thoughtless words. "Father is at rest," said this valiant young daughter of his. "He suffered much before he died, but now he sleeps peacefully. In Heaven's morning I shall see him again."

Never had I heard such an astonishing statement. Suddenly Teresa exclaimed, her voice shaking with emotion, "Surely, thou art a daughter of the good God and our very beloved Paula!"

The three days that followed Paula's arrival were very happy ones for me. I greatly wanted to take her to school with me, but my father thought that for a while she would be better in the house, where she could accustom herself to her new life and be with poor Catalina whose strength diminished day by day.

In the morning, and at dinner-time, and after school, and in the evening, we were always together. On my return from school, we took tea together out of doors. When I had finished my homework, we would dig together in my portion of the garden, and then as the summer days were long ones, Teresa would let us play outside until bed-time.

Of course, I showed Paula all our toys and dolls and the wonderful illustrated books that had been given me from time to time by relatives and friends. Paula was in ecstasies in this new world of books that opened before her. She touched my dolls one by one, looking at them with awe, examining their clothes, passing and repassing her fingers through their hair and exclaimed, "Oh, how beautiful! Never have I seen such things before!" Paula in her turn, showed us her treasures. They were not very numerous, but we could see our country cousin esteemed them very highly. With a trembling hand she untied a red-and-blue pocket handkerchief, and without a word placed on the table a portrait, a little black-covered book, and some faded flowers. I took up the portrait. It was that of a young man with smiling eyes, quite similar to those of Paula, and with that same kindness and sweetness in his face, so that it was not difficult to recognize who he might be. "It's my father," said Paula quite simply.

I wished at that moment I could have said something to comfort her but I could not find a word to say. Sobbing, I embraced her, and I felt her hot tears mingling with mine.

"Don't let us cry anymore," she said presently. "My father and my mother are the Lord's. Some day we shall see them in heaven, and we shall be with them forever; shall we not Lisita?" "Yes," I said, somewhat troubled.

"See my flowers," she said. "I picked them near our house in the morning just before leaving. Do you not see? Here are forget-me-nots, pansies and daisies. Poor little things! It is hard to recognize them, but I shall keep them always, and when I return to Villar, I will carry them with me." "But you will never return there," I cried, "you are to stay with us always. I never want you to leave us."

"Well, don't worry about that, Lisita. When we grow up, you will go with me to my old home. Uncle Peter and the man that rented the farm from father, promised me never to leave the place until I grew up and returned. So I made them a solemn promise that I would come back and take over the farm some day. Perhaps the cows and the goats and the rabbits will all be different when I go back. If you only knew how I cried when I kissed them all on coming away—they all know me so well. I wonder if they still remember me."

With a sigh, Paula put her flowers back carefully in the handkerchief, and then passed over the little black book to me. "This is my Bible," she said. "It was my father's for years, and he gave it to me on the day he died. See, he has written my name here on the first page."

I was hardly able to decipher the shaky signature of our Uncle John, but finally made out the following,

"To
PAULA JAVANEL
A remembrance from her dying father."

It was an old book with many loosened leaves. On each page were many underlined passages, some marked with pencil, others with ink, with small neat comments in the margins.

"This is my most precious treasure," said Paula. "Father had it in his hand as he breathed his last. I promised him to read from it every day of my life, asking the Lord's help to understand what I read. Although Papa is no longer here, still I obey him. I try to remember all that he told me. He was a wonderful man, this dear father of mine, and how he did love the Lord! My one desire is to be like him."

"Yes, but you are only a girl yet," I said to her.

"That's true, Lisita, naturally I know that, but father used to say to me, 'You're not too small to serve the Lord, Paula!' I read the Bible with him many times, and when we didn't have time to read it in the house, we took it to the fields with us and read it as we rested. Then as I watched the cows and sheep, I read the Book alone. And now you and I can read it together; can we not, Lisita? And I know the Lord will help us to make everybody else happy around us. I've never had a sister, and now that you say you wish to be my sister, my prayers are answered!"

Then after a long pause, she said, "Why don't you answer me, Lisita?" And she laid her head on my shoulder and fixed her great eyes upon me. How could I answer her? I had a great desire to tell her of the true situation. We all of us wished to be as good as possible, if that should please her, but we would never be permitted to read the Bible. I knew father would never consent to that. Yet how could I tell her that

things in our house were not as they were in hers—in that God
was never mentioned! Then I remembered a long discussion
our old servant had had that very morning with my sisters on
this subject, and Teresa ended the matter by saying, "She's
only a little girl, anyway, and she'll soon become accustomed
to do as we do. Besides your father will remember how she
has been brought up, and he has too good a heart to make the
poor child unhappy. Of course in the end the thing will finally
adjust itself. Poor little thing! How she would suffer if we
should bluntly tell her the truth that we live here in this house
like a bunch of savages."

As I searched my poor brain for a reply, Teresa without
knowing it, came to my help by calling me into the kitchen.
Upon any other occasion, I would have simply answered
without moving, "What do you want?" But now I was only
too glad to obey her immediately and so put an end to a
difficult situation. "I'm going to town," she said, as she put on
a clean apron. "Perhaps you and Paula would like to come
along." "What a lark!" I cried, as I ran out to tell the glad
news to Paula, and two minutes later we were ready.

Teresa looked us over from head to foot, reminding us that
the strings of our shoes hadn't even been tied, that our faces
and hands showed signs of an all-too-hasty toilet, to say
nothing of a lack of a comb in our hair. Finally, however, we
were on the road to town, happy to find ourselves in the cool
shade of the long avenue of linden trees that stretched away in
the distance. What a joy it was to have at my side this new,
wonderful companion to whom I would be able to open the
mysteries of the great shops and public buildings—marvelous
things which this simple country girl had never seen before in
all her life. What could be greater happiness for any girl of my
age!

Chapter Five

LOUIS' WATCH

When Louis returned at the end of the week, he was surprised to find Paula so happy and contented. He found her in the kitchen helping Teresa to dry the dishes. "One would think," said he, "that you had been with us for many months instead of a few days." Paula showed herself to be much more embarrassed in his presence than she had been with us. It may have been the school uniform that did it. But Louis, like the good-hearted lad that he was, did what he could to make her feel at home. Presently, out we went into the garden to play, not without an anxious look from Teresa, for she knew that when Louis came into any situation, he generally caused trouble. When, however, we returned with our aprons decorated with mud but still happy, the good old lady heaved a sigh of relief. The fact is, that when Louis played with us he always acted as he did with the boys at school. But no matter what happened, Paula seemed afraid of nothing. When it came to running races, Louis found to his great chagrin, that she could even beat him at this; and in other games if she happened to fall and hurt herself, she'd rub an injured knee with a laugh or sucked a stubbed finger without further comment, and go on playing as if nothing had happened. But in spite of entering wholeheartedly into all our fun, it was easy to see that our servant had well named her, "The daughter of the good God!" She was always ready to step aside rights, to recover a ball at whatever distance when a dispute arose to, "Who should get it?" or to look for a lost kite, no matter how thick the brambles might be. No wonder Louis was quite content to have such an accommodating companion! Then the moment arrived when we must go back to the house. That fatal time always seemed to arrive on the wings of the wind. Teresa seldom had any time to come and call us, but she relied on Louis, as he had a watch. Beside all that, we could clearly hear the hour strike in the great clock on Darnetal Church.

"Listen," cried Paula, woefully, "it's nine o'clock, and Teresa said we must go back to the house at nine."

"Oh, shut up," said Louis. (He had just started a thrilling new game of jumping from a high wall.) "I'll tell you when it's time to go home. Now are you ready? Hurry up, Paula, get the ladder. There it is, under the cherry-tree!" Paula obediently ran and returned with the required ladder, and helped Louis put it in position, saying at the same time, "But Louis, you know well that Teresa told us that we must be in at nine o'clock."

"Oh, yes, I heard it," said Louis ill-humoredly.

"Well, then we must go!"

"Oh, not yet, five minutes more or less won't make any difference."

"No, five minutes won't make any great difference, of course," said Paula slowly, "and it certainly is lovely here, but Teresa ordered us in at nine o'clock. I'll run and ask her if we cannot stay another fifteen minutes."

"Certainly not," sneered Louis. "Teresa would never give permission. Now, hurry up, you're first on the wall, Paula."

"No, I'm not going to stay. Teresa would be angry."

"No, no, never fear. Besides, she'll never know. I think she's out."

"Well, she'll know when she returns. She'll ask us what time we came in."

"Oh, you needn't worry about that," and Louis took out his watch. "I can fix that matter easily." We both looked over his shoulder at the watch, which by this time clearly pointed five minutes after the hour. Suddenly, we saw the hands of the watch begin to turn backwards. "Now," said Louis, "what time it is?"

"Half-past eight," answered Paula, lifting astonished eyes to her cousin's face.

"Well, if it's half-past eight why do you look at me like that?"

"Because I don't understand."

"What do you mean by saying you don't understand? It's all quite simple. If Teresa is angry, I'll tell her that we left the garden at nine o'clock; then I'll show her my watch."

"But," cried Paula, quite upset, "that would be a lie!"

"Nonsense, you foolish youngster, that's not a lie. We'll go from here at the dot of nine, according to my watch, of course, if she doesn't ask us, we don't have to say anything. Besides, I do it for you and Lisita, for if you were boys instead of girls, there would be no reason to return so early. Now, up with you. Yes or no."

"Not I," said Paula, with a heightened color. Louis was furious.

"No, you say? Oh," he laughed, "that wall's too high." Paula looked at the wall. It was certainly high, but he knew very well from past exploits that the height would not bother her.

"No," she said, "I'm not afraid to jump. Over in Villar, when I had to tend the goats, many a time I have had to jump from far greater heights than that to keep them from straying into our neighbor's pastures; but I tell you now, we promised Teresa to return at nine o'clock and I'm not going to disobey her."

Then it was that I joined in on the side of Louis. "If you're always going to obey Teresa, you'll never have a quiet moment."

"Then are you, too, going to stay with Louis?" Paula asked sadly.

"Of course," cried Louis, without giving me time to reply. "And now, go if you wish and leave us in peace. Get out of the way!"

Paula, who was seated on the lowest rung of the ladder, immediately stepped aside and soon Louis was on the wall.

"Now, it's your turn," he called to me. I followed my brother as Paula slowly moved away up the garden walk.

"I'm going back with Paula," I said to Louis. Then from the top of the wall, I saw her turn her head for one last look.

"Oh, let her go!" said Louis. "She can find her own way. I'm afraid the little fool is going to become impossible. Now, do as I do. But be sure and don't break your nose, for Teresa will blame me."

"You jump first," I said.

"Getting afraid, are you? All right, see me jump. One, two, three!" and down he went, in the middle of a pansy-bed, Teresa's especial pride and the object of her particular care.

"Oh, oh," I cried, viewing the ruin that Louis had made. "Now, won't Teresa be angry indeed!"

"Well, why should I care?" said Louis. "Why did she have to put flowers alongside of a perfectly good wall like this? Now, hurry up and jump. We'll fix it up and water it, and she'll know nothing about what happened."

"Oh, Louis, I'm afraid!"—Certainly the distance to the ground seemed enormous!

"What are you afraid of? I'll catch you if you fall. Don't be a 'fraidcat!'" Just at that moment I would have done anything rather than jump.

"I'm coming down by the ladder."

"No, you'll do no such thing! Now, come on; don't be a coward!"

Just at this moment we heard a voice calling, "Louis! Lisita!"

Louis turned to see Paula calling us from the bottom of the garden.

"And now what do you want?" cried Louis. "I thought you had gone home."

I profited this diversion to come rapidly down the ladder.

"I was almost at the house," answered Paula, coming nearer, "but I didn't go in because I didn't want to meet Teresa."

"Why not?"

"Because I didn't know what to say to her, if she should ask me where you two were."

"Well, wouldn't you have told her the truth?"

"Of course, I would have to tell her. That's why I've come back to look for you. I've run all the way. Oh, please come now; won't you?"

My brother seemed to hesitate.

"You know I hated to disobey," added Paula, with tears in her eyes, "and at the same time, I don't like to be a 'tattle-tale.' Won't you please come home now with me?"

Louis was a good-hearted lad in spite of his short-comings. Therefore, seeing his young cousin begin to cry, he said, "All right, let's go. Anyway, I can't play the way I want, especially with a pair of youngsters like you two. But, look here, Paula, you forgot the ladder. Take it away now, if you want us to play up to all your nonsense."

Paula, grabbing the ladder, simply said, "Oh, thank you so much," as she dried her tears. I went meanwhile and filled the watering-pot while Louis tried to restore the crushed pansies as best he could.

"There you are," said Louis, finally, "Teresa will never know." And off we all three raced for the house.

"And so you are back already," remarked Teresa as we invaded the kitchen.

"Back already!" said Louis. "It's more than a quarter after nine, but if it hadn't been for the country cousin here, we'd have been a whole lot later."

Chapter Six

IN THE MIDST OF DARKNESS

My father had not had much time to pay attention to Paula since her arrival; for on his return from his long trip he had found the head of the factory very sick. This had so increased his duties that he hardly had time in the morning to take a hurried cup of coffee, before going off to work. In the evening, he always went to see Catalina for a few moments, and then he shut himself in his room where he worked far into the night.

It was, therefore, with a sigh of relief that he sat down at the family table on Sunday morning to take breakfast with us children.

"Now, then, Paula," he said, turning to our cousin as Teresa served us coffee, "you haven't told me how you like your new family?"

Paula colored a little as she said, "Oh, I love you all very much, uncle mine."

"Well, that's a happy reply," said my father, "and we love you also, my little daughter."

The coffee had been served. Paula had been with us four days and she knew that we never asked blessing; but she never dreamed that anyone would hinder her from following her own custom which she still continued every meal. Without any hesitation, therefore, she repeated in front of my father, the words that had surprised us so at our very first meal. "The food which we receive, O Lord, may it be blessed in the name of the Father, and of the Son, and of the Holy Ghost. Amen."

"What's that you say?" said my father, hardly giving her time to conclude.

Paula, still on her feet, with her hands still joined for the prayer, fixed her great luminous eyes on my father. She was not smiling now, and I saw that she understood that somehow she must have displeased him.

"Answer me," demanded my father. "What were you doing?"

"But..."

"Repeat those words of your prayer."

Paula quietly obeyed.

"Where did you learn that?"

"My father taught it to me. We always prayed before and after eating." Paula said this with a trembling voice, trying to restrain her tears.

"Listen to me, Paula," my father said in a voice less severe; "I don't wish you to imagine that I'm angry with you. In fact, I'm glad that you want to remember your father and his words. That is all very well. But I simply wish you to understand that in the future you are to conduct yourself like the other members of my family. Do you understand, my little daughter?"

"No, uncle, I don't."

"No? Well, then, I must speak more plainly. Your cousins no doubt have already told you that in this house I will permit no word relative to religion. In the future that applies to you also."

"But, uncle dear!"

"That will do. When you come to more mature years you will be able to understand my reasons, and if you should desire it at that time I will give them to you. At present it is enough for you to know that you are not to pray anymore. Hand me the morning paper, Rosa."

We ate in silence, all except Paula who apparently couldn't swallow a mouthful. Our father with his eyes buried in the paper, paid no more attention to her. I had a great desire to cry without knowing why, for I couldn't possibly understand why my father's warning should make Paula so unhappy. Father had not punished her, yet, nevertheless, to see her stand there with a mixture of grief and fright on her pale face, one would have thought that she had been threatened with a most terrible misfortune.

Rosa and Louis made understanding signs to one another. Meanwhile to demonstrate my own sympathy, I tried to take my poor cousin's hand, but she withdrew it, and I understood that it was useless to try to comfort her.

"Uncle," she cried suddenly, "oh, uncle mine, please pardon me but I cannot, cannot obey you."

"What's this?" said my father, gazing at her with stupefaction and growing anger. Our surprise at this untoward daring of our young country cousin was so great, that even Louis dropped his spoon and forgot to eat.

We had disobeyed very often, especially Louis and I, and many times we had been punished for it, for disobedience in my father's eyes was the greatest of all crimes; but never had we dared to defy him openly.

"Paula, be quiet," cried Rosa, fearing the terrible consequences of such temerity.

To our surprise, my father, in spite of his anger, remained calm.

"So you don't wish to obey me," he said, fixing Paula with a cold and severe eye. "That's the first time I've ever heard such words from any child in this house. Tell me, my daughter, what do you mean?"

"Oh, dear uncle," she said, drawing quite close to father, "oh, oh, uncle mine, don't be angry, please. I do wish to obey you in everything. Oh, yes, in everything, everything! I promised my father to be good and to show everyone that I am a daughter of the Lord Jesus. But, oh, uncle, I must pray, and I must serve the Lord. My father told me so, and God Himself tells me so, for so it is written down in the Bible itself."

"I think," said my father, "you will find written in your Bible, these words, 'Children obey your parents.' And according to you, you ought to obey the Bible."

"Yes, I know that well, those words truly are in the Bible, but papa told me that I should always obey God cost what may. Oh, dear uncle, surely you wish to serve Him. The Lord died for us, and for this, of course, we love Him. And I thought that you loved Him too. I never knew that there were people in this world who did not love God. Oh, please let me pray, dear uncle. I beg of you, I beg of you. Papa, my dear papa, oh, if he should know that I could never pray anymore! I promised him I'd see him in heaven one day, and he'll be waiting for us there, waiting there for all of us, you, and Lisita, and Rosa, and Catalina, and everybody. Oh, please, please let me pray!" And Paula put her head on my father's shoulder and sobbed as if her heart would break.

"Oh, let her pray, father," implored Rosa in a low voice. "She is so young, she'll soon forget." We could all see that there was a great struggle in my father's innermost self, as a tender look came in his eye, as if he would say, 'Don't cry anymore. There, there! Pray if you wish.' But suddenly his eye rested on us and the stern look returned. He had forgotten us. If he gave way to Paula now, how about the discipline of the rest of his family? Besides, if he permitted her to pray, what would hinder us also from invoking that same holy Name? It was too much.

"Listen, I tell you," he said; "you must obey, and obey at once. This thing has gone too far already." The only reply that came was the sound of Paula's crying. "There, there," said my father, "Stop your crying. I know your religion perfectly, and once I was on the point of practicing it, but, as I said before, your religion teaches obedience to those who are over you."

Paula raised her head, and amid her tears she said, "Listen, uncle dear, I'm only a little girl, and I don't know much, and I can't explain to you what I wish to say. I know well that it is my duty to obey you, and so my father instructed me before he died, and when I disobeyed him, he punished me, but in my father's case—" and here she hesitated.

"Go on, go on," said my father.

"My father's will was also God's will. He used to say that he was my earthly father but that God was my heavenly Father, and that if he should die, God was to be my Father forever. And no matter what happened, or where I was, I must continue to serve God, no matter who endeavored to stop me. For it is written in God's Word, 'We should obey God, rather than men'."

I saw my father go pale with anger. "You're an insolent girl!" he cried. "And I have a good mind to give you a good whipping, to teach you to respect your elders."

Paula looked at him with surprise. "I don't understand, uncle. Those words are written in the New Testament."

"Show them to me," ordered my father.

Paula, glad to escape for a moment, ran for her Bible, which was always beside her in our little bedroom. As she crossed the threshold, Teresa entered to carry away the dishes. "What now? What's the matter?" said the old servant as she looked at Paula's tearful face. "What on earth have you been crying about, poor child?"

My father answered for her. "She's been guilty of most incredible impertinence."

"That's strange," said the old servant. "That's not a bit like her, with her happy, humble ways with all of us."

"That may be," said my father, "but it's just as I feared. She's got all the ideas of her father's family. She talks of nothing but God and the Bible and of her religion, and that's insupportable in this house."

"Oh, do go slow, sir," Teresa implored. "She's a mere child yet."

"Yes, but she must obey."

Teresa contented herself with a shrug of her shoulders, for she saw that my father was not going to yield. And now Paula had returned with her Bible in hand.

"And now," said my father, after a moment of silence, "let us see those words. Have you found them yet?"

Paula had paused, her hand turning over the pages of her Bible rapidly. "No, uncle, not yet, but I will find them soon."

Again there was silence. Teresa had returned to the kitchen, the door closing with a bang to demonstrate her displeasure. Nothing could be heard but the tick-tack of the clock, and the sound of the turning pages, as Paula, in spite of her tears, looked for the desired words.

"Here it is," she said at last, smiling in spite of her emotion. "See, uncle, here you are, at the fifth chapter of Acts, verse 29."

" 'We ought to obey God, rather than men!'" murmured my father two or three times, as he read the words of Holy Writ, while Paula looked at him with confident eyes, even though a few tears still lingered.

"Let us see, now, something of the context," he added. "Oh, yes, here it is," and he commenced to read aloud,

" 'And the high priest asked them saying, Did not we straitly command you that ye should not teach in this name? And, behold, ye have filled Jerusalem with your doctrine, and intend to bring this man's blood upon us. Then Peter and the other apostles answered and said, *We ought to obey God rather than men.'"*

Teresa, who had forgotten the tablecloth, came to get it, and smiled as she saw that happiness had again returned to Paula's countenance; for nothing pleased the good woman more than to find everybody in the house happy.

My father leaving certain directions relative to Catalina whom he had found very weak that morning, gathered up his papers, also the Bible, and started to go out.

"Uncle," Paula reminded him timidly, "you've made a mistake. You are carrying my Bible away with your papers."

"Yes, that is true, but I've made no mistake. I'm keeping your Bible now."

"And you will return it to me tonight, uncle?"

"And why tonight?"

"To read it, uncle, as I always do every night."

"Well, you're not going to read it anymore! My children do not read the Bible and they're not so bad. And I've already told you that from now on, you're going to live the same as all the other members of my family, of which you now form a part!"

"Oh, uncle, uncle!" implored Paula, "please leave me that Bible! It is the Bible my father gave me on his dying bed! Please let me have it, I pray you, my dear uncle! I will be good, and I will give you everything that I brought here from Villar. But leave me my Bible, please! Please! Leave me my Bible!" Paula sobbed, clinging to my father with a desperate courage.

Teresa, who had viewed this scene with dismay, did not dare to interfere. She came and went, pretending to arrange things here and there in the room.

For my part, I could not comprehend Paula's conduct, not being able to imagine why she should dare so much for her little old black book—I, who would have exchanged all my books for a new doll; but I would have suffered anything to help her now. And so in spite of all Teresa's signs for me to keep quiet and sit down, I took my father by the sleeve and burst into tears saying, "Papa, please give it to her."

My father turned and looked at me for an instant. Never had I seen him so angry. His face had become as white as a sheet. Suddenly throwing Paula off, who had been holding on to him on the other side, he raised the Bible over her head and with a thundering voice, he threatened her. "Will you keep quiet?" Paula appeared not to have heard him.

"Oh, dear uncle," she implore once more, extending her hands to secure her treasured book, "oh, uncle." In reply all I heard was a dull thud, and I saw Paula fall to the ground. Beside himself, my father had given her a tremendous blow on the head with the Bible.

Teresa rushed toward the child and carried her into the kitchen, turning as she did so toward my father. "Have a care, sir," she cried, her voice trembling with indignation. "Mark my words, you will repent some day of what you have just done."

It appeared to me that my father had already repented. He took his hat without a word and went out, and did not return until the evening.

* * * * *

"What a shame that Paula isn't a boy," said Louis, as soon as our father disappeared.

"Why?" I asked.

"Because she is so brave. Did you notice she stopped crying as soon as father hit her? In her place, you would have been crying yet."

"And you? How about yourself?"

"Oh, boys wouldn't cry for a little thing like that. I'm surprised, though, that father hit her."

"I'm surprised, too," said Rosa, "but, of course, she must learn to obey."

"I wonder what can be in this Bible of hers to make her love it so," continued Louis. "Anyway, what is a Bible? Is it a kind of prayer-book?"

"No," I said, proud to know so much, "it's not a prayer-book. At least I have seen Paula pray in the morning and at night. She kneels and closes her eyes and prays. She tells me that in the Book she learns how to be good and to serve God. Her father used to read it to her every day, and when he died she promised him to continue to read it."

"Poor Paula!" sighed Rosa. "There is something mighty fine about her. I wonder how all this is going to come out."

"I think she'll die," I said, trying to keep back the tears.

"Nonsense," said Louis, "she'll not die! Not she! Don't worry about that. In a few days she'll forget all about it. But I can't help feeling very sorry to see her so unhappy. Well, good-bye, Rosa. Don't cry anymore, Lisita. I'm going into the kitchen to see what's happened to poor Paula."

I followed him out and we found the kitchen empty. I went to our room and found Teresa seated on my bed with Paula on her lap. I heard Teresa say, "My treasure, don't cry anymore! Don't afflict poor Teresa who loves you so, and who loved your mother before you. Now, come, come, my angel, that will do. You will make yourself sick. See, here comes Lisita to comfort you."

But Paula continued crying, inconsolable, as she hid her face on the ample shoulders of our old servant. I came quite near her and stroked her hair, but I could not utter a word.

"Papa! Papa," she called, time after time.

"Your father's not here," answered Teresa, taking her tenderly in her arms. "What would he think if he saw his little girl in such a state?"

"Oh, I only wish father had taken me with him! If I could only see him now! You see, I promised him to read my Bible and now I cannot, for my uncle has carried away the only one I had—that wonderful Book that told me of God, and where my father had marked so many beautiful passages! Oh, papa, papa, do come! Your daughter needs you now!"

Teresa, finally seeing that it was useless to try to comfort her, limited herself to drying the floods of tears that still continued to flow. But finally, thoroughly exhausted, Paula at last became calm and listened tranquilly to Teresa's long story which we already knew so well, regarding the death of our mother and Catalina's terrible fall. And following this, she showed her that on account of these great misfortunes, instead of leading our father to seek the Lord, it seemed on the contrary to have hardened his heart. Thus he had become rebellious, and had made it an established rule in our home that not a word should be uttered relative to the Supreme Being. Then she added, "But don't you believe that he does not care for you! If you could know how many times he has said that you should lack nothing and should be treated as one of his own daughters."

"That is certainly true," said Rosa, who had entered during Teresa's narrative. "Father appears severe and this morning, of course, he became very angry, but he is very good-hearted after all."

"I did not know, I did not know," said Paula, as she bowed her head; "how my poor uncle must have suffered."

"Besides," continued Teresa, "who can tell but what your uncle will begin to read your little—what is it you call it? The Bible?"

"Do you think so? Oh, Teresa! Do you think he will read it himself?"

"Certainly I do, and why not? And when he has read it and found that it is a good book, I'm sure he will return it to you. So now, just calm yourself and don't worry anymore."

"But," questioned Paula, "do you mean to tell me that my uncle hasn't got a Bible himself?"

"Yes, he had one once, but I imagine that he must have lost it, for it's many years since I have seen the one that he had."

"Oh," exclaimed Paula, "what a wonderful thing if my uncle should read my Bible. For I am sure that he will come to believe in God as my father did, and then he will let me have my precious Book back again. My father, too, passed through great affliction. My mother also died, and then my two sisters, all three in the same year. Father told me that by thus passing through the fire he had learned not to fix his eyes on the things of this world, but to find his happiness in God. I don't know how to explain it very well, of course; but I did understand it fairly well when my father told me and showed me some of the precious passages in the Book that helped me to understand."

"I think I also understand," murmured Teresa, drying her own eyes on the back of her sleeve, as she turned to Rosa. "Rosa, you claim to be very wise. Tell me, where can one buy a Bible?" Rosa smiled, and said, "I'm not very sure, but I think in one of the book-shops one could find a Bible. I could find out in school tomorrow. I know one of my schoolmates has one."

"Good," exclaimed Teresa, "you must find out tomorrow morning. I've got an idea, Paula, a wonderful idea, so dry your tears. I must go tomorrow afternoon to the city, and if Rosa can find out tomorrow morning where a Bible can be found, we shall all four of us go and buy a new Bible there, and you can read it in your room and your uncle will never know."

"Oh, Teresa," cried Paula in a burst of gratitude, "what a good woman you are!"

"That's something I've never yet found out," said the servant with a dry smile.

Then suddenly we all saw that something had begun to trouble Paula. "What's the matter now?" said Rosa. "Are you not content to get a new Bible?"

"Oh, yes," said Paula, "but under such circumstances that would deceive my uncle."

It was here that Teresa broke in. "No, no," she said, "you don't understand. I'm going to buy this Bible with my own money, and I can do as I please. If I care to buy a Bible, it's no one else's business."

But there was trouble in Paula's eyes as she said, "I would certainly like to have a Bible, but uncle has forbidden me to read it. I can see from what you say that it would be easy for you to buy another and read it yourselves, but my uncle has prohibited me and that settles it. I simply can't be a hypocrite and deceive him. Dear Teresa, I do certainly thank you from the bottom of my heart, but, you see, you had forgotten what uncle said. Now, listen, the Lord Jesus is going to help me! There are many beautiful passages of the Bible that I know by heart, and there are plenty of the Bible stories that I'll never forget. All these I will keep in my memory, and then besides I shall pray every day for my uncle, that he'll soon return my precious Bible to me, and give me permission to read it. I know the Lord will hear me, if I obey Him and pray with faith. Dear Teresa, I hope you're not going to be provoked with me."

"And why should I be, my precious treasure?"

"Well, just because I didn't want you to buy me a Bible."

"No, no, dear, no; you certainly are right, and a whole lot better than we are." And we, together with our old servant, could not help admiring the honesty of our sturdy country cousin.

"Teresa!" It was Paula who broke the silence that followed the above discussion.

"What now, Paula?"

"Will you pray for me?"

"I," said the astonished Teresa.

"Yes, please, Teresa dear."

"My poor little Paula, I never pray for myself, so how could I pray for you?"

Poor Paula seemed at a loss. "Well, you see," she said, hesitatingly in a trembling voice, "I'm afraid to do it. You see, I don't dare forget God."

And so our good Teresa, in order to satisfy the poor child, promised to pray for her that very night.

"No," insisted Paula, "let's pray now."

Our poor servant looked around her in dismay.

"I—pray here! In front of you and Lisita and Rosa! Never! Besides, I wouldn't know what to say."

"Do you mean to say that you don't know, 'Our Father which art in heaven?'"

"Perhaps, but it's some time since I've repeated that prayer. I remember my poor mother. I used to kneel beside her and repeat it when I was your age. Once in a while since then, I have said my 'paternoster.' But it's been many years since it's passed my lips, and I haven't even thought of it for ages. No, no; it's useless. No, Paula, you pray for us. We certainly need it, but as for me praying—a poor sinner like me—I tell you it's useless.

But Paula was not easily discouraged.

"Teresa," and Paula put her cheek against the wrinkled one of our old servant, "you know that Jesus died for us, and do you mean to say, notwithstanding that, you are living like a heathen."

"What's that you say? Like a heathen?" cried poor Teresa.

"Yes, Teresa, like a heathen. My father used to read me missionary stories on Sunday and in these stories I always noticed that the heathen people live without praying to God, and that they didn't read the Bible, and that they didn't know how to sing any hymns, and they had no church to go to, that is, until the missionaries came. But we are different here in this house from the heathen because they had never heard of God." And then she smiled one of those lovely smiles that always seemed to spread a halo over her.

Poor Teresa, placed her well-worn hands over her wrinkled countenance, and said, "Paula, Paula, you certainly are right. So we are even less worthy of God's mercy than they are."

Paula looked down at her for a moment in silence and then, kneeling down beside her, said, "Teresa, you just pray with me, won't you? I know the Lord Jesus will pardon you, and He'll help you to love Him for He has promised to give you a new heart. I'm only a little girl, but He helps me and He hears me when I pray, for that's what He has promised, Teresa. Once my father taught me a beautiful verse, and when my uncle returns my Bible, I'll show it to you, but this is what it says, 'Him that cometh unto Me, I will in no wise cast out.'"

Poor Teresa, with her head hidden in her hands, could not reply.

"Do come and kneel with me," insisted Paula, pulling her by her apron. After a long silence suddenly Teresa fell heavily on her knees beside her bed. Paula up to this moment appeared to have forgotten the rest of us, but now taking both of us by the hand she invited us to kneel also.

"No," said Rosa, with an offended air, "I'll do no such thing."

"Nor will I." I said, a bit intimidated by my sister's refusal.

And so Teresa and Paula kneeled together, " 'Our Father which art in Heaven,'" commenced the clear voice of Paula. Slowly came the repetition, 'Our Father which art in Heaven,' and poor Teresa's deep voice trembled with emotion.

" 'Hallowed be Thy name.'"

" 'Hallowed be Thy name.'"

And now Teresa, gathering fresh courage, as the words of the great prayer began to return to her memory, the voices now mingled in the same majestic words from, oh, such different hearts—the one, pure and confiding, and the other now contrite and penitent.

Then, as they finished, Paula continued, "Lord Jesus, be pleased to bless my uncle, Teresa, Catalina, Rosa, Lisita, and Louis. Oh, bless them, Lord, and help them all to come to Thee. And bless me, also, and give me Thy goodness, for Thy name's sake, Amen."

"So may it be," sighed poor Teresa.

Paula opened her eyes, but closed them again as she saw that Teresa had not moved, and that she was struggling to add a prayer of her own. Then finally it came.

"Oh, my God, my God," murmured poor Teresa. "If you can have pity on a poor sinful woman like me, that has forgotten Thee for so many years, be pleased to pardon me, and change my poor wicked heart, in the name of Thy Son, Jesus Christ, Amen."

*   *   *   *   *

For a good while after that, Teresa made no allusion whatever to what had transpired in our little bedroom on that first Sunday after Paula's arrival; but we noticed a great change in her conduct. She did not work harder—that would have been impossible—neither was she more unselfish, for a more unselfish person than our dear old servant would have been hard to find. But the thing we began to notice was that she was more patient and tender in her dealings with us children, and more charitable toward the great number of our poor neighbors, who would come to the door from time to time to "borrow" food—these poor miserable neighbors whom she had despised on account of their laziness and untidiness. Beside all this, we saw no more of her days of bad humor and fretfulness. For instance, she treated our father with much more respect and listened without argument or impatience when, at times, he was unjust in his criticism of the house arrangements. Then we noticed also that all her little lies with which she tried to frighten us at times had completely disappeared.

In the cottages of our poor neighbors, there had existed an atmosphere of discouragement and desperation, brought on of course, through poverty and drink, and it was here that our good Teresa began to be known as a veritable friend. As she passed from door to door giving a word of encouragement here, or taking the burden temporarily from the shoulders of a poor tired mother there, we began to notice the under-current of a happy change in the atmosphere of these poor and destitute ones around us. It was easy to imagine that Teresa might be the cause of the change.

*   *   *   *   *

The day following, Rosa was sitting by the bedside of Catalina who complained of her usual headache, and Teresa had gone out on an errand.

Paula, a bit exhausted with her emotions of the day before, appeared to have lost all animation but soon her naturally happy nature asserted itself, and by the time my father returned from his work, she ran to meet him and opened the door as he entered, embracing him as if nothing had happened.

"Well, well," said my father, "I'm glad to see that you have recovered your good humor, Paula." A frank smile passed over Paula's face, but she said nothing. "And how has Catalina been today?" he said, turning to me.

"She has a terrible headache. Teresa is afraid she's going to be sick again."

"Poor girl! We must be especially careful then not to make any noise," and he turned to go into Catalina's room, but Paula denied him.

"Please, uncle, have you pardoned me?"

"What for, child?"

"For what occurred yesterday. Surely you remember, uncle. I was a bit stubborn about giving up my Bible."

My father looked down at her, surprised. "And now, you're perfectly willing that I keep it?"

"Oh, yes, of course, for I did not at all understand. Teresa tells me that you had no Bible, and you see I didn't know that. And she said that after you had read it, you would of course bring it back to me. I am so sorry that I appeared so selfish. Please, pardon me, won't you, uncle dear?"

"I've already pardoned you, so don't worry about that. So you like to read your Bible?"

"Oh, yes; indeed I do, uncle."

"Well, perhaps some day I'll return it to you."

It was not exactly a promise, but Paula was willing to content herself with that much.

"Oh, thank you, thank you so much, uncle," said Paula as she embraced him.

"And so you love me a little, do you? In spite of everything?" asked my father smiling, as he took hold of her chin and turned her face up toward his.

"Oh, yes, indeed; you don't know how much!"

"You do?" said my father. "Well, that certainly gives me great pleasure. I see that soon we shall come to understand one another, you and I. By the way, I noticed that in your Bible there were quite a number of dry flowers. If you would like them, I will return them to you immediately."

"Oh, many thanks, uncle. I kept them there as remembrances of my father. I shall keep them in some book where I can look at them often—often!"

"That's what I thought, my little daughter. I'll go and get your Bible, and you yourself shall take them out."

But now Paula seemed to have a different idea. "No, I think that I prefer that they remain where they are," she said in an altered voice.

"What's that you say?" exclaimed my father, astonished. "How is that you have so suddenly changed your mind?"

"Well, you see," explained Paula, trembling a bit, "they'd better remain where they are, for I love my Bible, and I've read it every day, and now if I saw it again, I'm afraid— I'm afraid—," and poor Paula's lip was trembling.

"I understand, I understand," said my father.

But on turning to go into Catalina's room, he hesitated with his hand on the latch of the door, and turning, he looked searchingly at Paula, as if he would know the secret of the innermost heart of this child, so loving, so angelic, and yet so absolutely natural.

Chapter Seven

CATALINA'S ILLNESS

Teresa had not been mistaken. Catalina became so critically ill during the following week, that my father lost all hope of her recovery. Not being able to be with her during the day, he watched at her bedside during the greater part of the night, and if it had not been for Teresa, who compelled him to go and take some rest, he would have, undoubtedly, suffered a collapse himself. How long those days appeared to be in spite of the happy companionship that I had found with my dear cousin Paula! My father hardly noticed us, absorbed as he was with the fear that filled his heart, and Teresa was occupied with so many tasks that she had no time for us either.

Rosa had to leave school in order to help nurse the sick one, and Paula also was required to stay home until the afternoon session. As for me, I was packed off to school in the morning, carrying my lunch in a little basket, fearing each night as I came back to the house that I would receive bad news as to Catalina. My! What grand resolutions for the future I made during those sad days—to try to love my poor sick sister, and to treat her better than I had done, should she recover.

One afternoon, I was surprised to find my father at home. It was only about five o'clock and he generally did not return from work until eight. He seemed so sad and depressed that I dared not embrace him as was our custom. Teresa crossed the dining-room and gave me her usual warning. "Don't make any noise, Lisita. Go and sit down and be quiet."

"Teresa," said my father in a low voice, "do you think Catalina would be able to see the children?"

"Why do you ask that, sir?" she said.

"I would like them to see her that she may embrace them for the last time. You know what the doctor said."

"Oh, those doctors!" said Teresa in a scornful tone. "The doctors don't know what they're talking about. Don't lose hope, sir. I know that Catalina may not live to be very old, but if God wills her to live, she will do so in spite of the doctors."

"Yes, but you know how weak she is. She never will be able to survive so many complications. And yet, how can I bear such affliction? She reminds me so much of her mother, the same voice, the same blue eyes, and even her identical way of smiling. And now to follow this child to the cemetery and return to the house where she will never be any more. Oh, what shall I do! What shall I do!"

"Why don't you consult the Great Physician, sir?"

"What do you mean by 'the Great Physician?'"

"I mean the Lord Jesus. Deliver Catalina into His hands. When He walked this earth, all the sick ones were brought to Him and He healed them all."

"But He's no longer on earth."

"No; but His power is the same today as it was then."

"Teresa, do you pray nowadays?"

"Yes, sir, I do."

"When did you begin to pray?"

"From the time that Paula entered the house, sir."

"I suspected that."

"Now, please don't go and rebuke her, sir. If you only knew how she loves you, and how she prays for you and Catalina. Oh, sir, how many times she has made me blush for shame."

"How so, my good Teresa?"

"That's a fact, sir. I used to think to myself, 'You're a pretty good woman, you have suffered much in your life, you work hard, you don't do any harm to anybody, surely you will go to heaven.' But when I saw Paula and the reality of her religion, and how she loved God, oh, then, sir, I comprehended for the first time in my life that I was a sinner worthy of death, and I prayed to God that He would pardon me."

"And—did He do it?"

"The Saviour assures us, sir, that 'He that cometh to Him, He will in no wise cast out.' So I dare to believe that He has pardoned me." Teresa was pale with emotion. It was the first time that she had confessed the Lord before men, and it cost her a good deal to do so to my father. He was apparently too depressed to be angry. After a moment of silence he said, "Where is Paula?"

"I sent her to the drug store, sir, to get certain medicines that the doctor ordered."

"When she returns, send her to Catalina's room. I shall remain there until, until—" My poor father could not conclude the sentence.

Then turning to me, "When Paula returns I wish you to come in to Catalina's room also, Lisita."

"Yes, father," I answered him in a low voice.

A quarter of an hour later Paula returned. Never shall I forget the anguish and terror that I experienced when Teresa, warning us to be quiet, led the way to the bedside of my dying sister.

Catalina did not appear to notice our entrance. Her eyes were closed, and her face so pale that I believed her already dead, but my father made signs to us to draw a little nearer and putting his hand over the forehead of my poor sister, he called to her gently, in a voice that betrayed his anguish,

"Catalina, Lisita and Paula have come to visit you. Would you not like to embrace them?"

"Lisita...Paula..." I heard Catalina murmur in a far-away voice. "Ah, yes, I remember. Help me up, father." My father lifted the poor thin body of his daughter. In spite of all I could do, I could not keep from crying, thinking that it would be the last time that I would embrace my big sister, whom I had loved so little. She looked at us for a long while, and then said calmly, "Have you two come to say good-bye to me?"

"No, no" said my father; "we hope that . . . "

"No, father, I'm dying. I know that well. It is useless to keep it from me. Think of it, only eighteen years old, and yet I've been of no use to anybody, and nobody's going to miss me very much."

"Catalina," exclaimed my father, "do not speak so. You hurt me talking that way, and you make Lisita and Paula cry."

"Are you really crying, Lisita?" And Catalina turned her feverish eyes toward me. "How strange! I have not been a very good sister to you, and I always thought you didn't care for me."

"Oh, Catalina," I exclaimed, kneeling beside the bed, "please don't die. I do love you so. I promise to come and care for you every day and I'll never make another noise while you are sick. I will be always good to you, indeed—even when you're bad-humored. Please don't die." And then I sobbed with such violence that my father, fearing that such conduct would cut even shorter that parting life upon the bed, asked Teresa to take me away.

But Catalina said, "Let her alone, father. It really does me good to see her cry. I never dreamed that Lisita had any heart at all. But I see now that it has been all my fault. If I had only been a bit better-tempered with her, she would have shown me a little more affection. Rosa, give me a little water, please." And Rosa placed a teaspoonful of water between the lips of our poor sister.

"Are you quite bad, my daughter?" asked my father.

For some minutes, Catalina could not reply, but finally she said, "Lisita, don't cry anymore, please. Now, listen."

I tried to calm myself.

"We need to ask each other's pardon, my poor little sister," she said.

"Now kiss me. Tell me that you forgive me."

"Oh, yes, indeed, I do forgive you," I answered, "from the bottom of my heart. It is I who have been wicked whereas you have been so very, very sick, while I enjoy such good health."

"Yes, that's true," said Catalina, "but I'm older, and I should have shown you a better example. I had always thought of myself and now—it's too late to change. Come, dear Lisita, come and kiss me once more."

I could have wished to have stayed there on my knees for hours and hide my head with shame and tears but I didn't refuse to show this last sign of affection for Catalina. So I laid my hot cheek against that of my sister, trying to bid her good-bye, and her tears mingled with mine.

When Paula's turn came, Catalina was so exhausted that she could hardly say a word. But finally, she said, "You will take my place at father's side, Paula. Father, I'm dying. Paula will take my place, and I know she will be a better daughter than I could have ever been."

Her strength was going rapidly and we could hardly hear her words. And now my father softly put her back on the pillows and motioned us to retire.

Exhausted by remorse and grief, I threw myself on my bed and continued crying until at last I fell into a heavy sleep.

*   *   *   *   *

During the week that followed, Catalina hovered between life and death and good old Dr. Lebon came and went two or three times a day. Teresa never went to bed, but took short cat-naps in her chair at times, as best she could, and my father made very rare and short visits to his office, bringing a good part of his work home with him.

Rosa now replaced Teresa, either in the kitchen or at the bedside of the invalid, as the case might be. And I continued at school where, thanks to the fears that filled my heart, I was a model of good conduct.

Paula had quickly learned to make herself useful. She lacked experience in a house like ours, but her willingness and cheerfulness more than made up for the clumsiness of her hands as she would say to Teresa, "Let me do that, dear Teresa; you are so tired, and you have so much work now." Teresa, accustomed as she was to perform everything herself, hesitated a little at first; but Paula would look at her in such a beseeching way that she generally yielded to her.

From the time that Catalina fell ill, Rosa had to make all the purchases in town, and this was not a small thing, for the distance from the old Convent to the city was considerable. At times Paula was allowed to go with her. "Why don't you let me go alone to the city?" Paula said to her. "If you did not have to go out, you could help Teresa so much more in caring for Catalina."

"That's true; but you couldn't go alone to the city. You'd get lost!"

"No, no, never fear such a thing. Let me go, and I'll have not a bit of trouble finding my way back." And Rosa, like Teresa, at last yielded to her pleading.

"How is Catalina now?" was my first question on returning from school.

"Always the same," Paula would say.

"Do you think, Paula, she'll ever get well?"

"That I don't know, Lisita. But I believe she will. Teresa prays for her, and so do I. God is able to heal all the sick people. You know that; don't you, Lisita?"

And then, as she thought of the dear sick one that the Lord had not healed, whose body was lying in the faraway Waldensian valley she added, "I know the Lord did not heal my father, but then, you know, he was *prepared* to go."

"What do you mean 'prepared'?" I said, a bit puzzled.

"Oh, I mean to say that my father had given his heart to the Lord Jesus, and so he was *ready* to go to heaven."

"I suppose it is very difficult to prepare one's self for heaven," I said guardedly.

"Oh, no," said Paula. "If we ask the Lord Jesus to give us a new heart, He always does so."

"What do you think," I said, "has Catalina received a new heart?"

"I don't know," and Paula hesitated, "but I don't think so. She torments herself so, and seems so afraid to die."

"Oh, Paula, how I wish she would get well! Before she became so ill, I didn't care for her a bit, and I believe she didn't care for me either. But after having said good-bye to her that afternoon, I certainly do love her. Poor Catalina! In the middle of the school session, many times it comes to me, 'Suppose that Catalina should die to today!' Then I do not seem to be able to pay any more attention to the lessons. It seems as if Catalina was there, dead in her bed, and I hardly dare to come home. If I had not been so wicked to her before she became so ill, I know I would not feel so."

"Now listen, Lisita! This is what you ought to do. You ought to ask the Lord Jesus to heal Catalina."

"He'd never do it for me," I said.

"And why not?" asked Paula.

"Because I'm sure God doesn't hear the prayers of wicked people."

For a while Paula did not answer me. I saw that she was thinking about what I had just said. Suddenly, a ray of happiness illumined her face with its great dark eyes, as she exclaimed, "Yes, He does hear wicked people."

"How do you know that?" I said.

"Because when Jesus Christ hung on the cross, one of the robbers asked Him to remember him when He came into His kingdom, and the Lord promised to do so."

"Well, then," I murmured, "perhaps the Lord might hear me also."

Paula turned about and faced me. "But, my dear Lisita, you're not wicked."

"Most certainly I am," said I.

"No, no, you're not that bad, and if you wish to be my sister, you will love the Lord Jesus, and you love Him now with all your heart; do you not, Lisita! I don't like to hear you say that you're wicked, for you are a good girl, and I love you dearly, Lisita!"

I? I? Good! I stared at my cousin. At any rate I knew that that very night, for the first time in my life, I was going to pray to the good Lord before I slept. Teresa had come in to say good-night and put out the light. I hadn't the courage to get up and kneel beside the bed as Paula did, but I joined my hands in prayer and closed my eyes as she had done, and with my head buried in my pillow, I murmured, "Oh, my God, I've never asked anything of You, and I wouldn't have dared to have said a word to You tonight if Paula had not said that You heard the prayers even of wicked penitent ones like me. My God, I ask You to heal my sister Catalina, and I ask it with all my heart. I haven't been very good to her, and I'm very sorry, and I'm going to be better from now on. My God, please let her live. I thank you ahead of time, Amen."

*   *   *   *   *

Two days later Catalina was out of danger! It was my father who told me the good news on my return from school.

"Oh, how happy, how happy I am, father!" I cried as I danced for joy.

"No more than I am, my daughter," he answered gravely.

Chapter Eight

THE FIVE-FRANC PIECE

Catalina recovered slowly and seemed to constantly desire Paula's company. In the afternoon, on returning from school, I would find her by the bedside, always happy, always smiling, with the complete forgetfulness of self that had always been such a wonder to me.

A new gentleness seemed to come over my father as the days passed, and I noticed that he always seemed to observe Paula with a sort of puzzled air.

Paula, too, seemed to change. That little Alpine flower, accustomed to the pure mountain air of her beloved country, naturally could not be transplanted from her native soil without some damage, and besides, that sensitive conscience of hers always seemed to be in a struggle between obedience to her God and her duty towards my father.

"That girl is nothing more or less than stubborn," I heard my father say one day to Teresa; which remark our old servant answered with a grimace behind his back.

One day, Teresa with an air of triumph, showed us a New Testament on her return from town. Paula took it from her hand for a moment, and then returned it to our old servant after caressing the shining cover with great tenderness.

"Take it," said Teresa, "it's not only mine, but yours, and you will have more time to read it than I will."

"No, Teresa, dear," and Paula sighed as she put her hands behind her back. "I know I'll get my Bible some day. That's what I've asked God for, and I know He answers prayer."

A little later, Paula said to me, "I certainly would have loved that New Testament, for there are two or three favorite passages with which I would like to refresh my memory, but I simply can't deceive my uncle. But what am I going to do, Lisita? I must never forget what I promised papa when he died." (Never forget, never forget—was Paula's constant preoccupation.)

But in spite of these problems which seemed to confront her, her perfect faith in God came to her aid, and seemed to give her wisdom to take the right road through it all. At times I would surprise her on her knees with her eyes closed and a certain strange indefinable light on her tear-stained face. Immediately however as she sensed my presence, she would spring to her feet and I found my companion. It was not in vain that she prayed! Her God, whom she had not ceased to serve in the midst of the worldly atmosphere that surrounded her, seemed to come to comfort and strengthen her.

Away off here in Villar, the little orphan, was not forgotten. One day, to her great excitement, Paula received a letter, directed personally to her, from someone from her own beloved land.

"What beautiful writing!" exclaimed Rosa. "Who could it be from?"

"I think it must be from my god-mother," responded Paula, trembling with emotion. "Oh, do give me the letter, Rosa."

Rosa, always full of fun, pretended to keep the letter, to the dismay of our small cousin, who didn't always see through our jokes, but finally yielded to her entreaties.

"Wouldn't you like to read it to us, Rosa?" asked Paula, tearing open the envelope. "I find it much harder to read writing than printing."

Rosa was only too glad to learn the secrets contained in such an unusual communication. And so this is what we heard as she read, "My dear god-daughter: I cannot tell you how dismayed I was on my return from Geneva to learn of the death of thy father. I know he was ready for heaven, but it is for thee that my heart was torn with anguish. Canst thou imagine the pain that filled it when I found on my return to Villar, that both of you had gone from me?

"The Pastor in the village told me that thou hadst gone to your uncle's house in Normandy, and that thou wert well-cared for. But oh, how I would have wished to have kept thee with me. But thou knowest, that for me, that would have been impossible, having to care for my old father and mother, as well as pay off their debts. I know, however, with the help of God, someday I shall be free. Then we shall return to buy the little farm where my father made us such a happy home, and at that time I trust that thou wilt come back and live with me— but then, I suppose thou wilt have become a great lady, and wilt not be content to come back to such a simple life with an obscure country woman (although I really don't believe that)."

"Oh, no, no, no!" suddenly interrupted Paula. "God-mother knows very well that I shall never forget the happy life in Villar."

"Then, you will go back there?" inquired Rosa.

"Of course. Why not?" and Paula looked quite surprised.

"What's that you say? You would leave all of us who love you so?"

"Oh, no indeed, you shall come with me," responded Paula, who generally had a way of solving every difficulty.

Rosa smiled and returned to her reading. "I have just been to see the grave of thy dear father where I planted some hardy white roses which will stand the winter winds. I went also to the neighboring village of Endroit where thou usedst to visit the poor, and immediately I was surrounded by thy friends. Papa Pierre Vigne especially sends his love. They all spoke of thee and called down blessings on thy head, especially that thou mightst be a witness for the Lord in thy new home. Mama Vigne recalled the time when thou visitedst her when she was so sick, and how happy thou madest her when thou didst sing those beautiful hymns to her. I believe, my dear one, that if thou shouldst write her a few lines, it would be like letting in a little heaven on her simple life, as she would thus see that the daughter of their best friend is thinking still of those whom she used to make happy by her heavenly presence. All those that have known thee and know that I am writing send kisses and loving remembrances. Many persons have asked that thou shouldst pray for them. They love thee so and miss thy presence, my dear, dear god-daughter! Continue, Paula, always to be obedient. Love everybody, and above all else, love the God of thy father. Love not the world nor the things that are in the world. Be thou a valiant soldier, faithful unto death, and Christ shall give thee a crown of life, for He will never forget thee, and neither do we in this far-off valley, nor thy good deeds which thou hast done amongst us. And now, may God bless thee and keep thee safe in His hands . . . Thy loving godmother, Evangelina, who prays for thee."

Paula, overcome by emotion, buried her face on Rosa's shoulder.

"What a minute," said Rosa, "don't cry. Here is something more."

Paula dried her eyes and listened intently as Rosa continued, "P.S. I am sending thee five francs by money order which you can redeem at your post office. Buy something with it by which to remember me."

"Five francs!" repeated Paula, with astonishment now instead of tears on her face, "Are you sure?"

"Of course. See. Here is the money order."

Paula, who never in her life had owned a single cent, could hardly believe that she was the possessor of so much riches!

Her godmother's letter was, of course, a tremendous event for all of us. Rosa had to read it over and over many times, and it seemed as if Paula wished to learn it by heart. Even my father read it with great attention and appeared quite pleased. Teresa declared that "The god-mother was surely a 'tres comme il faut'," but she did not explain to us why.

One thing, however, displeased Teresa—the eagerness with which Paula immediately planned to spend all her money.

"How now!" she exclaimed, "Is it burning a hole in your pocket? I should think a little girl like you would prefer to keep the money."

"Keep it?" said Paula. "Why should I keep it?"

But the next day, when Teresa announced that she was going to the city, she invited us both to come along. "What are *you* going to buy?" she asked Paula.

"Oh, so many things. You shall see!"

And the "things" which we "saw" were certainly a great surprise to us. First we went to the book-shop where a number of souvenir cards were purchased to send back to Villar. From there, on passing a window filled with fruit, Paula exclaimed, "Oh, my, Catalina certainly does love grapes. I must get her some."

"Grapes!" said Teresa. "Look at the price, you silly child."

"Never mind. I'm rich this afternoon."

"Well, you won't be rich long, if you make many purchases like that!"

But Paula would not be satisfied until a great bunch of the luscious fruit was safely stowed away in Teresa's bag, destined for Catalina. Having arrived in front of a stationer's shop, two pencils went into the bag, one for Rosa and the other for Louis.

"And aren't you going to get anything for yourself?" said Teresa, with a quizzical grin.

"Oh, you shall see," laughed Paula. "Besides you know, Teresa, I've got everything I need, and a good deal more."

But now a present for my father was the next object for discussion. "Men don't need presents," said Teresa impatiently.

But Paula did not agree with her. "I know," she cried at last, "I remember what he said yesterday that his coffee cup was too small. Let's get him a big one." So off to the china-shop we went, where a huge blue cup decorated with flowers of extraordinary size depleted Paula's treasure by a whole franc. I begin to ask myself whether I was going to have any part in Paula's generosity. But on passing a certain bazaar where a myriad of things were sold, I saw Paula make signs that Teresa seemed to understand. Contrary to her custom Teresa entered alone, telling us to walk on a bit and she would join us soon.

"And now," said Paula, "we must buy an apron for Teresa, while she's not looking. Where shall we go?"

"I think it would be better to let her choose one, and anyway, Teresa will soon be out of the bazaar and will be looking for us."

"Oh, my, no! This has got to be a surprise!"

"Yes, I know. But how are we going to work it?"

A moment later, however, Paula discovered a way, a bit risky perhaps, but the circumstances seemed to justify the means.

Teresa, suspecting that Paula's generosity would extend to her, and wishing to avoid that, watched us both carefully; but when all purchases appeared to be completed, the good woman occupied herself with buying provisions for the house, which of course entailed considerable discussion as to price, etc. It was then that Paula had her chance.

"Now's our time," she said to me in a low voice.

I followed her without delay. Teresa, meanwhile, argued the price of butter and cheese with an old school-friend, now elevated to proprietorship of the shop, and we knew that this would take at least a quarter-of-an-hour. We soon arrived at a place where they sold novelties, and where the clerks were about ready to close for the night.

"Oh, sir," cried Paula, to one of the young men, "will you not please attend to me? I'm in a great hurry."

"So, you're in a hurry," said the young man jovially.

"Yes, you see, we've run away and we've—"

"Wait a minute," said the young man, and he appeared to grow suddenly grave. "This is quite serious. Who have you run away from?"

"Oh, it's only Teresa across the street, and this must be a surprise for her. Will you please show me an apron?"

So the young man, without further ado, hauled down a number of these articles for inspection. "There you are. Take your pick."

Paula gave one look, "Oh, no; not that kind," she said with a consternation which I shared, seeing in imagination old Teresa with her great wooden shoes and her long skirts adorned with one of these elegant articles of the latest fashion.

"No? Don't you like these?" questioned the clerk.

"Oh, no," said Paula. "You see, it's for Teresa."

"And pray, who is Teresa?"

Paula started to explain, when the anxious face of the old servant showed itself at the door of the shop across the way, and not seeing us, had started to look up and down the street.

"Here she comes," I said. "Oh, Paula, what shall we do?"

"Go in behind the counter, there," said Paula who never lost her head.

I got in behind a pile of merchandise while Paula continued to explain her wants to the clerk from the dark corner of the shop. The young man appeared to comprehend our situation.

"Bertrand," and he turned to one of his fellow-clerks, "please attend to this young girl. I'll be back in a minute."

But "Bertrand" hardly had time to ask us what we wanted, when our first friend returned, bringing with him a package under his arm.

"I had a look at your Teresa," he said, "and I think that an apron of this excellent cloth will give her a thousand thrills. See, what beautiful stuff it is."

Paula gave a nervous look toward the window before answering.

"No, she's not there," said the young man, divining her thoughts. "Not finding you here, she's gone on a bit, but you can find her easily enough."

We were enchanted with the goods which he displayed, and we were soon served, at not too great a cost.

"You have been very good to us, sir," said Paula, starting to go out. "We have given you so much trouble, but when we wish to buy anything more, we shall always come here, will we not, Lisita? In the meantime, many thanks," and she extended her hand to him with surprising self-possession.

"The pleasure is all mine," said the young man, and I could see that he'd never met her like before.

Teresa was not far away, gazing into a jeweler's window. "At last, you're here," she said amiably. "Now, we must hurry for it is very late." She made no mention of our untoward absence and one would have believed that she had not noticed it, and that relieved us very much.

"You certainly are late," said my father to Teresa on our return.

"I thought we'd never get through," said the good woman. "For you see, Paula had to spend—"

"Oh, yes, I understand. She had to get rid of her five francs.

"And now, Paula, show me what you have bought."

"All right. Here you are, uncle!"

Paula had always shown a certain timidity toward my father, and appeared to be slightly afraid of him. Slightly red in the face, she took out the packages one after the other from Teresa's bag.

"You shall see, sir. You shall see," commented Teresa, with a shake of her head.

"What a lot of packages!" said Rosa, on seeing all the bundles tied up with such care.

"Shall I help you open them?" said my father. "Let us see what's in this first package. My, my, what's this? White grapes! And of the finest kind! You certainly have got good taste. I'll say that much, Paula!"

"They are for Catalina, uncle."

"For Catalina?"

"Yes, uncle dear."

Now there was not a sign of derision in my father's voice. It had changed to a surprising tenderness as he said, "So you brought this for our Catalina? I know the cost of such fruit, and Teresa should not have consented."

"And do you think, sir," broke in Teresa, "that when Paula wants to buy something, that she asks for my consent? You will soon be able to judge that for yourself. I never saw her equal."

"And this?" questioned Rosa, taking up the package of souvenir cards.

Paula indicated the destination of each one as she gave the name and address of many of her old neighbors in far-away Villar.

"So you don't forget your old friends," observed my father.

"Oh, what a beautiful box this is," continued Rosa, "and, oh, look here," as she displayed the thimble inside. "Who can this be for?"

"Oh, that's for Lisita."

"For me," I cried, jubilantly, "oh, Paula! So you remembered that I have just lost my thimble."

"Two pencils," announced my father, undoing another small paper package.

"One of them is for Rosa and the other is for Louis," said Paula simply.

"My poor dear child," exclaimed Rosa. "What on earth are we going to do with you! Here's another package but it appears so fragile that you'd better open it yourself."

"No, no; that's for uncle. Let him open it."

My father cut the cord that held the package. Paula hardly dared to raise her eyes, as he took the beautiful cup with its blue and gold ornamentation and took it over to the fading light, in order to examine it more carefully.

"I don't know whether I should be angry or content," he said, with a dry smile.

"Better be content, uncle," said Paula appealingly.

"Well, so be it," he said. "At any rate, I am happy to have such a good generous niece, who does love her uncle a bit. Is it not so, Paula?"

"There's one more thing," I cried. I wanted to see the effect on Teresa of that final package, which Paula handed over immediately to the old servant, saying gently, "It's for you, Teresa dear."

"What's this? How is it for me? When I strictly forbade you? But there you are! What can one do with such a girl?"

The apron was found to be eminently satisfactory, and Teresa promised to put it on first thing in the morning, and I could see a few tears in her eyes as she said so.

"And now," said my father, "You've shown us all these things which you have bought us with your five francs. Where is the present for yourself?"

Paula looked at us with dismay.

"I declare," she said, "I forgot! Never mind, I can buy something tomorrow." And she held up a few small coins which were all that remained from her five-franc-piece.

My father looked at her searchingly, with that new tenderness which I had seen frequently lately, and then left the room without another word.

"I believe," said Rosa, "that she'd be happy to give us her last piece of bread if there was occasion for it."

"Yes, and her life also, if that was necessary," said Teresa in a shaky voice, as she turned back to her duties in the kitchen.

Chapter Nine

A LITTLE GLIMPSE OF HEAVEN

What a wonderful afternoon it was! The sun far down in the west, painted the eastern mountains with a lovely tint of orange. The warm air was balmy with the perfume of flowers and the birds were singing cheerfully as they flitted about.

All was quiet in Catalina's bedroom, where Paula and I were seated. My sister was now on the road to partial recovery, having passed the danger-mark some days before. Another change also I noticed had come over her. Her impatience and irritability had gradually disappeared, day by day, and when she suffered more than ordinary, she never seemed to complain. The expression of her face had sweetened also, and even a slight but quite natural smile would often illumine her thin features. Death had passed her by, but now seemingly a new influence gradually possessed her. This simple country maid of the Waldensian mountains had come smiling into her life and although Catalina had frequently abused the kindness of our cousin, Paula never had lost patience with the poor invalid. Soon love had triumphed, and Catalina had begun to return the love of her little nurse even though at times she still kept her tyrannical attitude.

"No," she answered, "She's a 'Daughter of the good God!' Just as I said one day when she first arrived." Teresa sighed as she added, "What would I give to be like her!"

One beautiful afternoon, the poor invalid lay there with her eyes on Paula as if she wished to say something.

"How do you feel now?" said Paula as Catalina's fixed gaze seemed to disturb her somewhat.

"Oh, I'm all right just now. I was thinking of your godmother's letter. She remembered, she said, the hymns you used to sing. You've never sung any of them to us, Paula."

I saw a mist in Paula's eyes as she answered. "No, that's true. I don't think I've sung a note since my father's death. Would you like to hear me sing?"

"Yes, indeed," said Catalina, without noticing Paula's emotion.

I was on the point of reminding them of father's formal prohibition relative to hymn-singing, but an imperative sign from Catalina stopped me.

"What do you wish me to sing?" said Paula.

"Anything you care to. It's all the same to me."

"Then," said Paula, "I will sing to you, 'No Night There'."
And then to our unaccustomed ears came the glorious words:

> *In the land of fadeless day,*
> *Lies the city four-square,*
> *It shall never pass away,*
> *And there is no night there.*

> *God shall wipe away all tears;*
> *There's no death, no pain, nor fears;*
> *And they count not time by years,*
> *For there is no night there.*

Paula had that rare gift, the "golden" voice, a voice that seemed to penetrate to one's very soul. Catalina was enchanted!

Suddenly, I heard the heavy steps of a man coming along the corridor. But as Paula began the second stanza, I heard them pause.

"All the gates of pearl are made,
In the city four-square,
All the streets with gold are laid,
And there is no night there.

And the gates shall never close,
To the city four-square,
There life's crystal river flows,
And there is no night there."

Paula's voice trembled at the beginning. Then presently the sadness in her tones disappeared, and they seemed to swell out like an echo of radiant happiness. Catalina listened, hardly breathing. Involuntarily, I asked myself if Paula in heaven would be any different from the little country girl I saw seated near the window at this moment. I had an instant's impression that a man was standing behind the door, but I felt this could not be, for I knew that my father would be at his office. A special light came over the expressive face of Paula as she continued:

"There they need no sunshine bright,
In the city four-square,
For the Lamb is all the light,
And there is no night there."

And then again the wonderful refrain:

"God shall wipe away all tears;
There's no death, no pain, nor fears;
And they count not time by years,
For there is no night there."

The sweet sounds died away, and Paula looked smilingly at Catalina as if asking her opinion of the song.

"What a marvelous song!" exclaimed the poor sick girl. "And, Paula, you have a voice like an angel!"

I did not hear my little companion's reply. This time I was not mistaken; there was someone behind that door. Impelled by curiosity I ran to open it. At first I saw no one in the darkened passage, but finally I could make out my father moving off down the hall. When he saw that I had discovered him, he stopped and put a finger to his lips, and made signs to me to keep silent, but in my surprise I cried, "Is it you, father?"

"Yes," he answered, "I came home earlier than I expected. Was that Paula who was singing in Catalina's room?"

"I—, I—don't know," I hesitated, not knowing what to say.

There was an instant of terrible silence like a calm before the storm.

"You—don't—know," my father slowly repeated. "You dare to look at me and say you don't know when you have just this moment come out of your sister's room?"

"Oh, father, please forgive me," I exclaimed penitently. "It was indeed Paula that sang. But don't punish her. She didn't know that you had forbidden our singing hymns."

"Who said I was going to punish her?" my father questioned. And I could see that his anger had cooled. "Come here!"

Taking me by the hand, we went back together to my sister's room.

"Would it tire you, Catalina, to hear Paula sing again?" he asked.

"Why, no, father," Catalina answered, surprised.

"Then, Paula," said my father, "sing again that same song."
And once more we heard, "There's No Night There."
"Who taught you to sing?" my father asked.

"I think it was my father. But in our valley, everybody
sings. On the roads, climbing the hills, caring for the animals,
in the meetings; in fact, everywhere."

Catalina looked at my father furtively, and noticed that his
face remained serene, almost tender, and so she hastened to
profit by the occasion.

"Dear father," she said in a low voice, "Let her sing to us
once in a while; will you? It's such a joy to hear her."

"Doesn't it tire you?"

"On the contrary, I think it does me good." And Catalina
looked at her father appealingly.

"Let her sing," he said, "but leave it to the nightingales to
sing along. There are so few of them."

"And won't you let the crows sing along with her, too, if we
care to?"

"There are too many crows," said my father, shaking his
head.

"You are right, father, and your daughter Catalina is one of
the number, for she's only a poor sick crow. But sometimes,
father, you know that crows envy the nightingales."

The comparison made my father laugh heartily, and he let
himself be persuaded by his elder daughter—that elder
daughter whose voice was so like that of that dear wife of his,
now forever silent.

"Well, crows and nightingales let them sing together," he
said; and embracing all three of us, he bid us good-night. He
disappeared, but not without turning for a moment to Paula
with a remark, "Good-night, my little Alpine nightingale."

And Paula, who did not seem to comprehend a single word of this conversation, answered gravely, "Good-night, Uncle."

Chapter Ten

IN THE COUNTRY

Once a year we were accustomed to visit our grandparents
and this was generally made a real family reunion. There we
met with all our uncles and aunts and cousins. It was also a
joyful occasion for Teresa who was very fond of Justina,
grandmother's faithful old servant. Grandfather had been a
very successful farmer, intelligent, hard-working, and
economical without being stingy. After many years' work he
had amassed a considerable fortune. The big farm which to
Catalina and Rosa was but a dim memory, but whose glories
Teresa had often recounted to us, had been sold quite a
number of years before. My grandfather had then bought a
beautiful house nearby, with a few acres surrounding it just to
remind him of his former activities. The garden itself was
large and imposing and well-cared for under the critical eyes
of both of our grandparents, who specialized in new and rare
plants. The flowers, appearing in profusion in all seasons of
the year (even in winter in the great hot-houses), filled the air
with their delicious perfumes.

Our grandparents reigned over this domain and it was here
that they loved to welcome us. Our father was their especial
pride and joy as he was the oldest son.

Our grandfather had a gruff enormous voice and possessed
a pair of great square shoulders; in fact, he was a real
"countryman." But beneath his rude exterior he had a heart of
gold, and no one could gain the confidence of a little child
quicker than he.

Grandmother was of a different type with her long black
dress and her beautiful white hair, of which she was justly

proud. She could easily have been mistaken for a noblewoman. She was a strong character and had had the advantage of considerable schooling. She was every inch "the fine lady," with her firm step and resolute voice and her brilliant black eyes. Nevertheless, we all loved her dearly, for there was a simple loving heart hidden away beneath all her magnificence.

Justina, who had been her faithful servant for forty years, never tired of singing the praises of her "Madame." If during our short stay at "Las Lilas" we showed ourselves unduly boisterous, or when we disobeyed orders, Justina would say to us after we had been properly reprimanded, "You never, never will be like your grandmother!"

Grandfather always met us at the little railway station. On our arrival he embraced everybody, including our father whom he would kiss on both cheeks as if he had been a child. Catalina would first be hoisted up into the great carriage and we would follow one after the other. Louis took unto himself the honor of holding the reins, and after everybody was well-seated, except my father and grandfather who marched on ahead of the horses, the slow procession to the house would begin.

In half-an-hour we could see the great house where grandma and Justina, decked out in their Sunday gowns, awaited our arrival. There, after various comments on our growths and states of health, Catalina would be conducted by her grandmother to her room to rest after the tiresome journey, while Justina would carry off Teresa to the kitchen, and the rest of us would hurry to the orchard where grandfather with a vigorous hand would shake down the apples and pears into our outstretched aprons. Those were ecstatic moments when we could bury our teeth in the newly-fallen fruit. Soon father would cry, "That's enough! That's enough! There'll be nothing left for anybody else!" But grandfather continuing to shake down more fruit would answer with his great gruff voice, "First come, first served! Besides, look over there to the right! There are thousands of apples that we haven't even touched!"

Soon after this there would appear in a cloud of dust, the carriages of our uncles August and Edward with their families from Havre and Paris, carrying all sorts of bundles mixed up with children and nurses.

In the doorway of the garden would be our grandmother waiting to welcome everybody, her numerous grandchildren clambering about her and embracing her affectionately, each one fighting for the first kiss. "Me, me, grandma; I'm the smallest." "No, me, me, grandma; I'm the biggest." When they had been all finally satisfied, she would embrace with great tenderness all her sons, inquiring of each in turn as to his health.

Sometimes in the conversation there would come a cloud of sadness as some relative would be mentioned who had departed since the last family reunion. Then finally, after having returned to the garden to play for a while under the great trees, the bell of the nearby church would strike the hour of noon, and Justina would appear at the grape arbor entrance crying, "Come one, come all! The soup is getting cold!"

Then there would be a wild race on the part of all the cousins to see who would be first at the long table placed in the cool shade under the great spreading vines; that wonderful table with its wide damask covering which only appeared on state occasions. Grandma's loving hospitality was shown in the minutest details of that elaborate feast; for she had remembered the favorite dishes of each one of her three sons and each found himself confronted with the delight of his childhood. When under the maternal eye in the bygone days, he was not allowed to overeat; but now each was left to his own discretion to satisfy the most ample appetite.

And then came those delicious desserts followed by fruits and nuts, which had been especially kept as the crown of the feast to accompany the final coffee-cup. Again the afternoon was spent in the garden, while the babies slept in the shade under the eye of the respective mothers.

The most solemn moment of our visit was when we had to make our report to our grandparents as to our progress in school. I remember especially one year when Rosa was the first in her class, and Santiago our tall cousin had taken the first prize in the great school of "Louis the Great," from which each year he carried new laurels. For them it was of course a time of triumph—but for me! Oh, with shame I presented my report card. My grandmother read it. "Lisita Dumas,—last place!" and I hid my face in my hands.

"Come, come," grandma said, "don't cry. Try to do better next time."

My cousins were not quite so charitable as they passed my poor card from hand to hand.

"Tell us, Lisita," Santiago said, when he thought we were well out of ear-shot of our elders, "you certainly do love to ride the seat behind, do you not?" and he pulled my hair with that remark, "Better let somebody else sit there, hereafter." But grandmother overheard him and she said, "Go a little slower, my fine fellow. Lisita might have a more brilliant future than you think. And besides, when you, my fine grandson, are scintillating in the world of letters and Rosa is director of the great normal school, perhaps Lisita may be occupying a comfortable post right here in this great house." I didn't understand the full import of these remarks, but I noticed it had the effect of silencing my tormentor who slunk away abashed.

We would play happily in the garden until supper-time and even the grown folks joined us in some of our games. Sometimes father would gather all of us children around him, and we would never tire of hearing the stories of his adventures when, as a young man, he had gone far beyond the boundaries of France. These wonderful stories seemed so strange to us as we looked upon our father's sad and severe countenance; but our uncle August and Edward informed us that one time he was the happiest and gayest of them all.

After supper came the problem of housing us all. The boys always slept in the hay barn. "A good preparation," said Uncle August, "for their future training in the army." The rest of us found resting-places somehow here and there in the great house. On the following day we would gather at breakfast, and then the men folks would be off again to their various tasks in the big towns. After a good time in the garden in the morning, the two carriages to Paris and Havre would be loaded up again, and we would take the train once more, generally leaving Catalina to pass an additional week in the invigorating air of "Las Lilas." This short visit in the country was the great event of the year in my young life. I talked about it six months beforehand and for six months afterward. The other scholars made fun of me in school, and dubbed me "Las Lilas" because I talked so much about my grandfather's home in the country. But Paula was a most sympathetic listener. She never tired of hearing me repeat over and over our experiences at "Las Lilas." It must be confessed that I exaggerated in describing many things about my grandfather's place, until my country cousin came to believe that my grandfather's house was a palace and that the garden was a veritable Eden.

"You shall see, you shall see!" I exclaimed as I ended my description.

The cow appeared to be the most interesting thing to Paula. "If your grandfather has a cow, it must be that he really lives in the country," she said.

"Of course he lives in the country," I said, "it is so beautiful there. But don't you think that we also are living in the country here in "The Convent?" Paula laughed heartily at this but made no further comment.

At last the annual letter of invitation arrived. I recognized it on account of the beautiful handwriting of my grandmother. "It is for next Saturday," announced my father, "and we are all invited to stay until Monday. And now listen, Paula, this concerns you. Grandmother writes, 'It would delight me very much to embrace our new little relative. I hope that from now on she will keep a warm place in her heart for her old grandmother who loves her without having met her'."

Teresa, who was indeed tired out with the care of Catalina, and who was very sensitive to warm weather, was no less happy than we were, for she, too, was to go with us. Only Catalina manifested no enthusiasm over the coming visit. My father observing this said to her anxiously, "You have nothing to say, daughter mine?"

"I'm not going, father."

"What's that you say? You've been much better these last days and are well able to stand the trip. You weren't very well last year, and yet you went to 'Las Lilas' and found it so beneficial to your health."

"Yes, I know, father," answered poor Catalina, "but I know also that I've always been a source of great trouble for you, and Teresa would never have a minute's peace because of me. I shall go a little later, father, when I'm stronger, if grandmother will have me. She knows very well how I long to go to 'Las Lilas' but I fear that the trip would only bring on an especial spell of weariness and that would spoil the fun of everybody. Maria, who works in the garden here, can look after me for a day or two. She is very kind and thoughtful, and I know she'll care for me very well."

We all stared at Catalina! It was the first time in all her history that I had ever seen her forget herself. It was a great struggle, for she had become so accustomed to think only of her own comfort. Tears welled up in her eyes as she smilingly awaited father's decision. "But this is going to be a great disappointment to you," he said, passing his hand over the feverish forehead of the invalid.

"No, father; it will give me great pleasure this time," came Catalina's brave answer.

"Be it therefore as you wish," he said.

Pleasure? I couldn't understand what pleasure there would be for Catalina to stay behind alone with Maria, especially at this time of the great event of the year.

My father looked at Catalina tenderly as if he read her very heart, and saw there something he had never seen before. "Thou hast changed much, daughter mine, since your last sickness."

"For better or for worse?" asked Catalina with a mischievous smile.

"For better, my daughter. Indeed far better!"

"It's because I'm older than I was, perhaps, father."

"No, no; it's more than that."

"I wonder if I could dare tell you the truth."

"Never fear. Tell me what's on your mind, Catalina."

"Well, it's this, father dear. God has spoken to me and I have answered Him."

"How has He spoken to thee?" said my father, and there was no sternness in his look either.

Catalina pointed furtively at Paula.

"And how hast thou answered Him?"

"I've asked Him that He might save me and that He might make me a real Christian."

There was a strange look in my poor father's face as he answered quietly, "If I could believe that there was a God, I would say that He had heard thee."

Catalina wrote a long letter to grandmother, the contents of which she did not care to show us. So it was as Catalina wished, and Maria promised to take good care of the invalid.

At last the great day arrived. Paula and I, up at sunrise, scurried to the window to look at the weather, and oh joy! It was a magnificent day without a cloud in the sky! A little later when Teresa arrived to call us, great was her surprise to find us all ready to start.

"What a wonderful thing," she remarked dryly, "you'd never be late to school if you did this every morning."

After the first moment of enthusiasm, Paula strangely enough began to lose little by little the happy atmosphere which usually surrounded her. I discovered soon the cause. She was thinking of Catalina.

"It's going to be terribly lonely for her," she said.

"Never fear," I said, "she can go another time."

But she shook her head as if trying to throw off something painful that seemed to be on her mind.

"Oh, Lisita, if you could but know how lonely Catalina will feel as she sees us go without her. When I took her breakfast to her yesterday and saw that she had been crying I simply could not bear the thought of leaving her at home alone."

"But if papa says it is all right, it can't be so bad. Besides father loves her as much as you do."

Paula didn't answer me.

Soon the time came to start. Teresa started calling to one and another. One had lost this thing, another had misplaced something else. My father scolded and helped, at the same time trying to get us off. Then Rosa wasn't ready and Louis, always unprepared, couldn't find his favorite blue necktie. At last we were ready. The only thing that remained was to say good-bye to Catalina. Louis, impatient to be off, performed that ceremony quickly; Rosa who had reserved a surprise for the invalid, put a new book into her hand as she kissed her; Teresa, as she embraced her in her turn, left many instructions; then, as Paula came forward, we heard a sob as she buried her face on my oldest sister's shoulder.

"What's the matter now?" said my father. An unintelligible sound was heard, but Catalina understood and her eyes moistened with happiness. "Oh, father," she said, "I know; she's crying on my account, she doesn't want to leave me alone here." "Is that it, Paula?" questioned my father. "Yes, please leave me here, uncle, I shall be so happy to be at Catalina's side while you are gone." But Catalina refused this sacrifice, saying, "No, no, my dear little Paula. I'll not be lonely. You have too tender a heart. Now go, things will be all right here. Everything has been arranged for me, and it will make me happy to know of the good time you are all to have with our grandmother."

My father didn't know what to do. The time was passing. "Come, Paula, come," he said; "it's time to go."

Paula raised her head. "If you order me to go, I'll go, for I must obey you, and I know they are waiting for us. But if you will *permit* me to stay"—and she put emphasis on the word *permit* in her peculiarly irresistible manner—"I would be a whole lot happier here than in 'Las Lilas'."

"Stay then," said my father, as he added with a smile, "You certainly are a little despot, for you seem to twist me to your will in everything."

Paula laughed at this, as happy as if she had received the most valuable of gifts, as she kissed him.

"Oh, yes; kisses are all very well," said my father, pretending to be angry, "but what will the grandparents say?"

"You will tell them"—but the rest of the sentence I could not hear, as she bent close to my father's ear.

"Where's Paula?" everybody cried, as we went through the door downstairs.

"Look," said my father, pointing to the upper window. There was Paula, with a radiant face, waving her handkerchief in good-bye to all of us!

"Come, come, hurry up; stop your fooling!" cried Louis.

"I'm staying here."

"How is that?"

"Oh, I'm just staying with Catalina."

"That's too much!" cried Louis, "to stay here while the rest of us go on a holiday. Papa, you won't permit such a silly thing; will you?"

"Well, she begged me with tears to let her stay and there she is," said father.

"Good-bye, uncle; good-bye, Teresa,—a happy journey to you all," cried Paula. "Give a good hug and a kiss to grandmother and grandfather," we heard her say as we turned the corner.

"She isn't a bit like the rest of us," said Louis, "she never seems to seek her own pleasure, and yet the funny thing about it is, she's always happy. I can't understand a nature like that."

"It's because she finds her happiness in making other people happy," said Teresa.

This was also what our grandmother said, when we explained Paula's absence.

Chapter Eleven

THE CAT MOTHER

It was the month of October. I was sure that my father would permit Paula to go to school with me after the summer vacation, but not so. Catalina herself wished to teach her at home. This decision caused me many tears and complainings.

Teresa tried to console me. "Don't worry," she said, "just wait a little. I know Catalina, she'll soon tire of teaching, and then she'll let Paula go to school with you." Teresa was right. In the beginning Catalina was enchanted with the task. Paula was obedient, and she did the best she could; but she didn't learn very quickly, therefore Catalina soon tired, and Paula, with a teacher so inexperienced, became sleepy and inattentive.

So it was that the teacher tired the pupil and the pupil tired the teacher. Catalina was the first to complain. "Paula doesn't care much for study," she said to her father. "I'm afraid I am wasting my time trying to teach her."

"Well, then," said father, "perhaps the best thing will be to send her along to school with Lisita."

Catalina hesitated a moment. She wished to do something for others, but she was slow to learn how.

"I think it would be better to let her go," she said resignedly.

So it was that the following Monday my father accompanied us both to school and duly inscribed her as a student. Paula immediately became the center of great interest on the part of my school-companions. They remarked upon the beauty of her eyes and hair, the latter reaching almost to her knees.

Coming out of class at noon-time all forty-five pupils surrounded her affectionately, and at the end of a week Paula was the best-known pupil in the entire school. Catalina was

106

right, however, for Paula was not really a student, but she applied herself because, as she said, she did not wish to cause pain to Mademoiselle, the teacher.

As she left the school in the afternoon, the teacher would kiss Paula with a tenderness not seen toward others. At times Paula would bring her a few flowers, which caused Mademoiselle's eye to sparkle with such happiness that she almost seemed beautiful to us.

"Have you a garden?" she said to us one day.

"Yes, Mademoiselle."

"How happy I should be to have one. When you have an over-abundance of flowers don't forget me."

"Poor Mademoiselle Virtud," said Paula one day, "I am sure she has some secret burden."

"Nobody likes her," I said. (I remembered that I had twenty-five lines to copy because I had talked all the afternoon.)

"God loves her!"

"And you?" I questioned.

"Oh, certainly," said Paula.

"Notwithstanding she is so disagreeable?"

"I do not know. We don't know her outside of school."

"And I don't want to know her. As for you, you love everybody that nobody else loves." And that was true: Paula was always the friend of the poor and the despised. In that great school which was a world in miniature, there were many unfortunate little ones who suffered neglect from their drunken parents; others were cruelly treated at home, and in the case of still others, their timidity or physical weakness exposed them to the ridicule of their comrades. In Paula, however, they all found a friend and a companion who loved them and defended them.

The capacity to love and to make the others happy, extended itself also to the animals, but not to those small boys who destroyed the birds' nests or threw stones at the horses and dogs,—these she attacked without mercy. In the neighborhood of "The Convent" where we lived, there were quite a number of this type of boy whose greatest pleasure was to torture the dogs and cats. One of these especially, the son of the "Breton," was a veritable executioner. He never attended school, for his father never bothered with him, and his mother, poor woman, accustomed to misery and the blows of her drunken husband, had apparently lost all semblance of human feeling. This boy spent his time tormenting anything or anybody who was unable to resist him—old men, sick people, little children, and especially dumb animals.

One cold day in December Paula and I were walking slowly along the street, studying our lessons as we walked. Suddenly we heard the piercing cries of a cat in distress. Paula, always touched by suffering of any kind, stopped to listen. Louder came the cries of the cat.

"Mee-ow, mee-ow."

Paula threw her grammar on a road-side bench. "Poor little thing," I cried, "we can't help him, for I can't see where he can possibly be."

"Well, I can't stop here," said Paula. "Come along, we'll soon find him."

We ran over to the canal which ran along a few feet below the avenue. Suddenly I was afraid!

"Perhaps Joseph, the Breton's son, is mixed up in this!" I said trembling.

"Come along anyway, unless you want me to go alone," Paula said quietly. So I followed her.

Sure enough, it was the Breton's son surrounded by a dozen ragamuffins of his own set. They took no notice of us. He had a beautiful black cat, that had a string tied to its hind legs. The boy was swinging it around his head and at times ducking it in the canal while his companions danced around him with delight.

"Now that he's good and wet, let's bury him," suggested Joseph.

"Alive?" said his comrades.

"Of course alive! And the old dame, his owner can"—

But here Paula suddenly lunged forward, seizing the wicked youngster by the wrists with surprising strength for one of her age.

"You'll do nothing of the kind," she cried. "Let him go; do you hear me?"

"Let me alone!" said the young bully as he tried to bite her.

Not being able to accomplish this, he gave her a ferocious kick, which caused Paula to let go with a cry of pain. She now saw that her efforts were useless.

"See, here," she said to him, after a few seconds' thought, "If you give me the cat, I'll give you four cents."

"Ah, you haven't got four cents."

"Yes, I have; I have it here in my pocket."

"All right, let me have the money."

"No, no," said Paula, " if I give you my four cents first, I know you will never let me have the cat. Come, give him to me," she said beseechingly; "he's never done you any harm and you have made him suffer so much." But Joseph refused this appeal. With a diabolical grin he raised the cat again to swing it over his head. There was a meow of agony—but it was the last one! In spite of her former lack of success, Paula made one supreme effort to rescue the cat. Somehow the string got loose, the cat escaped, and was soon lost to view.

Then the rage of the young ruffian knew no bounds as he turned to Paula.

"Run, run!" I cried; but Joseph and his companions cut off the only path of escape.

Crazy with terror, I began to yell, "Help! Help!" with all my strength; but the boys drowned my cries with their own shouts. This very circumstance saved us. I saw someone coming to our help.

We soon recognized with joy that it was Dr. Lebon. On seeing him the boys ran away with the exception of Joseph, who was a little too late. The Doctor, who knew him, suspected he was the guilty one, and succeeded in getting him by the ear. Then the doctor said to me, "What has happened, Lisita?" And I told him the whole story.

"Well, he won't do it again; that's one thing certain," said the doctor.

"Oh, let him go!" said Paula generously.

"Paula," said the doctor with a severity we had never seen in him before, "Go back to the house with Lisita!"

We had nothing to do but obey. On the way back we could tell by Joseph's cries that he was having a bad time of it!

Teresa was frightened when she saw the condition of Paula's leg, as the result of the terrible kick she had received. The doctor soon arrived at the house, and Paula could scarcely help crying as the doctor examined her; but he said as he left us, "If I am not mistaken, Joseph will never trouble you anymore."

This was true. Joseph avoided us for a long time; but he took revenge on us through the other boys, who would cry after Paula as she walked up the street, "Cat mother! Cat mother!" This incident won us a friend. Shortly afterwards, returning from school, an elderly woman that lived in one of the most miserable huts among the "Red Cottages," stopped us and asked if one of us was called Paula.

"This is she," said I, pointing to my cousin.

"Then you are the one that saved my cat," she said. "How can I ever thank you enough, Mademoiselle? For that cat is my one consolation. If you would be kind enough to visit me sometime, I would be so pleased to see you."

Paula looked at her in surprise, and said, "I will ask Teresa if we may come to see you." Which permission Teresa readily gave.

"It's Louisa, I know her well. She has lived in that little hut for fifteen years. True, she is a bit weak in the mind, but she would never hurt a fly. Speak to her of the Lord Jesus, Paula! It will do her good."

On the following Thursday, therefore, we went to visit her. As we left the house, Teresa handed us a jar of preserves, saying, "Give Louisa this. Poor thing! Not many good things have come into her life."

Louisa herself answered the knock, "Ah," she said, "please excuse the disorder. If I had known you were coming today I would have straightened things a bit. Sit down here, on this box, Mesdemoiselles. I am sorry that I have no chairs to offer you. Ah, here comes Cordero!" she continued, and we could hardly recognize the beautiful black cat that jumped purring into Paula's lap, as the same cadaverous animal that was swinging around Joseph's head a few days before.

"It's my one friend," said the poor old woman, sitting down on another box.

"Do you believe that?" said Paula. "Can you not call us your friends? And there's another friend who has sent you a present. Our Teresa sent this for you." She placed in the eager hands of the old woman the preserves.

"Is it for me? How can I thank you? For years everybody has made fun of me, for I never speak to anyone; preferring the company of animals to that of people."

Paula had such a sympathetic way of getting at people's hearts, that instinctively she understood how Louisa had been.

"By the way," said Paula, "this is for your cat"—and she put two cents on the table.

The old woman did not seem to understand.

"It's for him, you know," said Paula, "you can buy some liver with this. Surely Cordero likes liver!"

The pleasure in Louisa's eyes was almost childlike, as she addressed her cat saying, "You must thank this good mademoiselle," and Cordero jumped down and rubbed against Paula in a most affectionate manner.

It was time to leave as the short day was ending and we had to be in the house before dark.

"How can I thank you, mademoiselle?" said Louisa. "Do come to see me soon again, even though I a poor old woman who nobody loves."

"Oh, Louisa," exclaimed Paula, "there is One who loves you: don't you know Him?"

Louisa shook her head sadly.

"No, nobody loves me. And to tell you the truth, I don't love anyone else either."

"The Lord Jesus loves you, Louisa."

'The Lord Jesus? Tell me about Him, mademoiselle; I have heard the name—who is He?"

"The Lord Jesus is He who died on the cross, that you might go to Heaven. He suffered much before He died. They despised Him. They beat Him. They spat in His face. Even His own friends deserted Him and He was so poor that He didn't have any place at night to lay His head. Yet, He was God Himself. He died for our sins,—and He rose from the dead. He is now in Heaven, and He waits to receive you there, Louisa. None of us deserve to go to Heaven, but He who was so perfect suffered in our stead. He died for all of us sinners that we might be pardoned. I wish I could explain it better, much better, but Jesus loves you, Louisa. I know He loves you more than you could ever dream."

Louisa's wrinkled face lighted with a smile; but she did not seem able to believe or comprehend this good news, which came to her, oh, so late in life.

"Oh, if it were only true," she murmured, as she clasped her hands together and her eyes filled with tears.

"But it is true, Louisa; don't you believe it? See here, He knows very well you live here alone with your cat, and that you are so sad, and that you have nobody else to care for you. He wishes to be your Friend, and He will be if you will ask Him. Why not ask Him right now, Louisa?"

"Oh, perhaps so, some day, mademoiselle."

"Do it now, Louisa."

"No, no; not now."

"Oh, why not now, Louisa?"

"Because I don't understand very well, mademoiselle. How could God love me, a poor, forlorn, useless old woman, who never loved Him, nor served Him. You come back again. Perhaps I'll end up by understanding better. And now, good-bye, mesdemoiselles. I have delayed you both too long."

We shook hands with her. Oh, what a cold hand it was! The touch of it sent a shiver through me!

"Goodbye, Louisa," said Paula, and suddenly kissing her, she gave her a hearty embrace as well and added, "I am going to pray for you, dear Louisa." One could see that the poor old woman was greatly touched as she said simply: "Thank you, mademoiselle, thank you."

I had almost forgotten Louisa and her cat when a few days later a neighbor came in with a worried look asking for Teresa. When she appeared, the woman blurted out the news that Louisa was dying.

"Louisa dying?   Nonsense, I saw her on the street yesterday."

"Perhaps so, for she dragged herself around until the last minute. But I knew she was ill, so I took her a cup of hot soup this morning. I found her in bed with a terrible cough, and now she can scarcely breath.   She keeps calling for Mademoiselle Paula."

"Have you sent for the doctor?"

"No; she's afraid he'll send her to the hospital and they'll take away her cat."

Teresa shrugged her shoulders.

"I'll go at once, and I'll take Paula with me."

Murmuring her thanks, the woman left.   "Can't I go?" I said. "Oh Teresa, please let me go too."

Teresa hesitated. "All right, come along!" she said at last.

Louisa's neighbor had not exaggerated her condition. The poor woman was sitting up in her bed. Its thin covers could not protect her from the cold, and a terrible cough racked her thin frame. When, at times, the cough left her she would fall back on her pillow completely exhausted. It needed all Teresa's efforts to restore her.

"My poor Louisa!" said Teresa tenderly.

"You were very good to come," said the neighbor who was staying as a nurse. "And Mademoiselle Paula?"

"Here she is. Come here, Paula."

And as Paula came near the bed, Louisa said with a weak voice, "Now I understand the love of God, for when you kissed me and embraced me, it was that kiss that made me understand that God loves even me. I will soon be far from the living, but I shall die in the arms of the Lord Jesus."

"Now, don't cry," continued Louisa weakly, as she saw us all weeping. "My misfortunes have been my own fault. I was selfish, I wished to live alone without God and without hope. I have been abandoned. I have known what it was to be cold and hungry for many years; but that happiest time of my life has been these last three days. They began with your visit, Mademoiselle Paula. That afternoon I prayed, and I believe God had pity on me. I am sure of that."

Here Paula broke in: "You had better not talk any more now, Louisa. Your cough will come back—you are already too tired."

"Perhaps so," Louisa said, "but I must speak while I have the strength for it. Oh, Mademoiselle Paula, I did want to thank you before I die!"

"But Louisa dear," said Paula in the midst of her tears, "I have done nothing for you; I didn't even know you were ill."

The poor sick one took Paula's soft hand between her thin ones, and raised it to her lips, "You have been like God's angel to me."

"No, no, Louisa, Louisa!"

"Yes, and you loved me, mademoiselle, and your love revealed to me God's love! May He bless you richly!"

"Amen," sighed Teresa.

Then again came that terrible cough which seemed to tear the poor weak body in two.

"I can do no more," she murmured, as soon as she was able to speak.

"Well," said Teresa, "you will soon be with the Lord Jesus."

A contented sigh came from the bed as we caught the words, "Oh, what happiness!"

"Is there nothing you would like us to do for you? No word to send to some friend or relative?"

"I have no other friend but Cordero, the cat. What will become of him?"

Teresa hated cats, and we never dared bring one into the home, but now we saw a struggle going on within her, and finally she said, "Would you be happy if we took him home with us?"

"Oh, indeed, yes," said the poor dying woman, "but please don't take him yet. Leave him with me until the end. He has been my only comfort and the nights are so long."

Louisa, however, did not remain alone any longer, for Teresa and several kind neighbors took their turns night and day to care for the poor invalid. Teresa brought from home pillows and blankets, and had a good hot fire always going in the grate. Dr. Lebon was called immediately, but it was too late; he could only make her last hours more comfortable. A few days later she died in Teresa's arms. A beautiful smile on the yellow wrinkled face gave it a happy expression that had never been seen there before.

Chapter Twelve

A TREASURE RESTORED

Our birthdays generally passed without celebration, either in the form of presents or parties, principally because my father disliked holiday festivities, as they seemed to bring back to him more bitterly the loss of her who could no longer share their joy with him. On New Year's Day, however, he always gave a little gift to each one of us. It was our custom to write in turn "A Happy New Year" letter.

Louis would always come from school to visit us during his New Year's holidays, and we had quite a number of visitors who bored us dreadfully. For me it was a time of good resolutions, and I would go to Teresa and say invariably as I embraced her, "I wish you a very happy New Year, Teresa. Will you please forgive me for all the trouble I have caused you this past year? And this new year, I am going to be very good." Unfortunately Teresa never saw any change.

As Christmas-time drew near, Paula questioned me to how we celebrated the day.

"We don't celebrate it," I said.

"Oh, Lisita, is that true? You do nothing special on that day?" questioned my poor cousin surprised.

"No, Christmas with us is not nearly so important as the New Year. Oh, yes; I generally have to put on my Sunday dress, and then I can't play, for Teresa is afraid I'll soil it."

"Oh," said Paula whose great eyes seemed to contemplate an invisible splendor. "In my country we always had a Christmas-tree, and celebrated the birth of the Lord Jesus."

"Tell me about it," I said, "I have heard about these Christmas celebrations, but have never seen any."

117

"Well," said Paula, "sit down here, close to the fire, and I'll tell you what we did last year. Four of our men went to the mountains and cut down a beautiful pine tree. They had to go up to their waists in snow, and what a job it was to bring it all the way down to Villar. But they were all very strong. My father was one of them. They dragged the tree into the church because there wouldn't have been room for everybody in the little school-house. We all helped to decorate it with gold and silver nuts, and we hung apples and oranges everywhere on its branches. But the beautiful part were the candles. There were hundreds of them in blue, green, red, white and yellow. If you could only have seen how beautiful it was, Lisita, when the candles were lit, especially when they crowned the top of the tree with a lovely white angel. We sang the wonderful Christmas hymns. Then the pastor gave us a fine talk about the Saviour. At the close, each of us children was given an apple, an orange, a little bag of sweets, and a beautiful little book."

"Oh," said I, "how happy I should be if father would let us go to see it all. It must be a beautiful country!"

"It is the most beautiful in the world," Paula assured me, her eyes sparkling.

"We too shall go and live there when we grow up; shall we not, Paula?"

"Yes, indeed, Lisita."

"You know, Paula, father always gives us a New Year's present," as I saw tears come into Paula's eyes as she thought of her old home. "What would you like to have if you could choose?"

"There's just one thing I want," said Paula, "and that's my little Bible."

"But that wouldn't be a present," I said.

"No, but it would give me more pleasure than any present," sighed Paula.

* * * * *

New Year's Day dawned with splendid weather. It had snowed during the night and the whole countryside was dressed in white. The sparrows flew back and forth under our windows, seemingly remembering our custom to scatter crumbs for them on such an occasion. Of course, we soon satisfied their hunger.

In the dining-room a huge fire burned, and Teresa with Rosa's help prepared the New Year's breakfast. Paula helped Catalina to dress, for Catalina, contrary to her custom, decided to breakfast with us, although against Teresa's advice, for she feared such early rising would tire her too much for the rest of the day.

"Yes, but I wish to be on hand when father distributes his New Year gifts," our invalid said. So Teresa had to yield.

Our father was late in coming so Paula ran to tell him that breakfast was ready, and soon back she came with her hand in his, with that affecting grace that was so habitual to her.

When he had received our "Happy New Years", father asked us if we wanted the presents before or after breakfast.

"Before! Before!" we all cried.

"Very well," he said, "I have tried to satisfy everybody's taste, so I trust everybody will be contented. Here, Paula this little package is for you. Catalina assured me that this would give you more pleasure than anything else."

Paula took the package and turned it over and over.

"It is a book," she said in a voice that was none too steady.

"Do you think so?" said Catalina with a smile. "In that case hurry up, and show us."

"Hurry up," cried Louis, handing her his jack-knife. "Cut the string and open the package. We want to see what it is."

She obeyed, a bit confused to see all the eyes fixed upon her. Inside she found a little black book with a much-used cover.

She raised her eyes in gratitude to father and tried to thank him, but could not find a word to say. Eagerly her fingers turned the precious pages. Suddenly out fell a five-franc-piece.

"There, there," said my father, as she tried to express her thanks, "I am more than satisfied, if I have made you happy."

"Happy!" said Paula, "I am more than happy!" She took her beloved Book, and as she turned its pages she found still other treasures—a few faded flowers which to my mind appeared to have no value whatsoever, and yet I could see that they seemed to call up once more the precious memories of her past life in that far-off Waldensian Valley.

"Dear uncle," said Paula, "Did you read the Book?"

"Yes, I read part of it, but if I have returned it to you today, it is not because I have finished reading it, nor is it because Catalina has begged me to return it to you. It is because you have obliged me to read another book."

"I, uncle? What book can that be?"

"Yes, it may seem strange to you, but you see, you have lived among us in such a way that I am to confess that I wish that my three daughters would imitate your manner of living. You have made me comprehend the love that your Bible speaks of, and of which Christ gave us an example, and which He apparently has put into your life, and so I give back your Bible to you with all my heart."

One can imagine our feelings as we listened to this strange discourse from the lips of him who only a short time before had been so opposed to such things!

"And then, Paula, I have something more to say," said my father. "Do you remember the day when I hit you on the head with your Bible as I took it away from you? I wish to say that I am sorry beyond expression for what I did that day—and now have you pardoned me, little daughter?"

For reply Paula took my father's hands in hers, then in a flood of generosity and forgetfulness of self she gave her Bible back to him, simply saying, "I give it back to you, dearest uncle!"

"You give it back to me!" said my father, stupefied, "You give me back the Bible you loved so much!" "Yes," answered Paula, "because Teresa has promised to give me another."

"But do you mean to tell me that you would care for a new Bible as much as this one?"

"Oh, no," she said, "Father gave me that one, and it's full of his markings, and it was in that Bible that I learned to love the Lord Jesus."

"And then—?"

"Well, it's because it is the most precious thing that I have in all the world that I give it to you. Because you see I love you so, and I would wish...Oh, how I do wish that you could learn to know Him too."

"My poor dear child," said my father, "I cannot accept your sacrifice, but I shall always remember your thought of me; and in the meantime, if you like, we can go out and buy another Bible like yours that I, too, may read it. How will that do?" At this Paula clapped her hands in delight, as she said, "Indeed, that will be wonderful!"

Chapter Thirteen

THE SCHOOL-TEACHER AND HER BROTHER

"Lisita," said Paula to me one day on returning from school, "Mlle. Virtud was not in class this morning."

"That's all the same to me," I said with indifference, "except that if I had known that, I would have gone to school anyway in spite of my chilblains."

"Do they still hurt you so badly," Paula asked.

"Yes, quite a bit; but not so badly as yesterday, and it bores me terribly to stay at home alone. You see, Teresa makes me clean the spinach, and Catalina gives me a basketful of stockings to darn, and I think I'd rather go to school, especially if there is anything the matter with the teacher, even though my feet hurt worse than a toothache. Do you ever have chilblains?"

"No, I don't think I ever had them."

"Well," I said, "I always seem to be the one that gets something—something that's bad and horrible."

"I think Mlle. Virtud is sick," continued Paula.

"You're always thinking of that woman. I tell you, it doesn't make any difference to me what happens to her," I said impatiently.

"Oh, Lisita, aren't you ashamed to say such a thing?"

"No," I said, "How do you expect me to like her? No matter what I do in the class she punishes me for the slightest thing; and not only do I suffer in class, but I get twenty-five lines to copy after school, so that I have not time to play with the rest of them. How I do detest that woman!"

"Of whom were you speaking?" asked Teresa, who appeared at that moment.

"Of the school-teacher, Mlle. Virtud."

"I have a good mind to box your ears," cried Teresa indignantly. "You detest such a fine young lady who works in your behalf."

"Oh, Teresa, don't be angry," I said. "You have no idea how she makes me suffer. When you were little you never went to school, so you do not understand. Now, listen,— instead of keeping the bad children after school, she sends us all home with twenty to fifty lines to copy, while she goes calmly back to her house. The other teachers keep the bad ones there for ten minutes or so, and that's all there is to it, which is a whole lot more agreeable."

"Mlle. Virtud is absolutely right, for she makes the punishment fit the crime."

"No, it isn't that," I answered in a rage; "It's because she doesn't want to stay in school like the other teachers, selfish thing! Here I am right now with lines which were given last Monday, and I'm not going to do them. She can say what she pleases!"

Paula, whose tender heart would have loved to have been on my side and also on that of Mlle. Virtud at the same time, suggested that perhaps she had someone who was ill in the house.

"She," I cried, "Mlle. Virtud! Who do you think would ever have such a disagreeable thing in the house with them! Besides, she has told us that her family live far away in the country."

"I don't know," said Paula; "but do you remember the day when we saw her carrying flowers back home with her. I dare say it was for somebody."

"Perhaps," I answered indifferently.

That afternoon Teresa permitted me to go to school, and there I found the teacher of the Third Year in charge of our class. She was a beautiful woman with lovely golden hair and blue eyes, and pink-and-white cheeks that reminded me of a wax doll. "Ah," said I to myself, "how I wish I was in the Third Year to have such a beautiful teacher always in front of me!" She read to us and told us stories almost all the afternoon, and never punished anybody, and on coming out of school her two little brothers ran to embrace her affectionately. "Hurry up, dear sister," said one of them, "Mama is waiting for us on the porch."

"My! How beautiful she is," I murmured to myself. "How I do love her! Mlle. Virtud would never be so gentle with her brothers, if she ever had any." Then suddenly I stopped, for it seemed to me that I heard Paula saying to me sadly, "Are you not ashamed of yourself, Lisita?" And I looked up to see Paula exchanging a few words with a poorly-dressed child just before she joined me. "Lisita, it is true," Paula said, "Mademoiselle Virtud is quite ill; she tried to get up this morning and wasn't able to raise her head. Victoria, the little girl who was speaking to me just now, knows her very well; in fact, she lives in the same courtyard."

"Who is taking care of her?" I said.

"No one, as far as I can find out. Do you think Teresa would let us go to se her?"

"No, I am sure she wouldn't, and for one thing, I'd never go. I haven't done my fifty lines."

"Oh, but see; I'll help you do your fifty lines right now."

"Oh, but that wouldn't be square."

Paula laughed, "You generally haven't such a delicate conscience. You know very well that half of the time Rosa does your lines for you."

"Oh, Paula, I swear to you—"

"No, don't you do anything of the kind. It's useless, for I've seen it myself, and I'm sure teacher would say nothing if I were to help you in order that we should both be able to see her. I'm sure she would be so delighted, Lisita. When my father was so ill, all his pupils came to see him, and he was so happy."

"You father wasn't like Mlle. Virtud though. Never! Never! I'll never go to see her."

"The Lord Jesus said that when we go to see the sick it is as if we visited Him. Wouldn't you care to go for love of Him, Lisita?"

"Well, we'll talk about that tomorrow," I answered, not daring to refuse on such grounds, and not caring to promise anything either.

Teresa gave her permission, and promised herself to visit the sick one at the very first opportunity. Paula wrote exactly half of my fifty lines, and in order to do so she sacrificed her playtime that afternoon because she wrote so slowly. I performed my twenty-five without further murmuring, and, exacting a promise from Paula that she would go in first, I decided to accompany my cousin on her visit to the teacher.

"Take this," Teresa said to us at the last moment. "It's just a little chocolate for the sick one, for there is nothing better to fortify her strength."

"Oh, many thanks," said Paula. "You think of everything. By the way I've got four cents; what do you think we could buy with them?" Teresa reflected a minute. "Get some oranges, and see that they are good and ripe. Don't stay late, for the days are getting short, and it gets terribly cold when the sun goes down."

Paula herself suddenly became very timid as we entered the Rue Blanche and asked a young girl where Mlle. Virtud lived.

"Ah, you are looking for Mademoiselle," said a childish voice.

"It's you, Victoria," Paula cried, "I'm so glad to find you here. Yes, we are looking for Mlle. Virtud."

"Come along, then," said Victoria as she blew on her hands that were purple with the cold, "I'll take you to her door." She took us up four flights of stairs when at last we came to Mlle. Virtud's apartment. "Here you are," said our little guide, and downstairs she went. I started to follow her down. "Oh, Lisita," cried Paula; "remember your promise."

"Well, why don't you knock?" I said, rather wickedly, as I saw that Paula was having trouble to muster up her courage.

"I don't know what's the matter with me; I can't seem to do it."

In a sudden spirit of mischief I suddenly ran to the door and gave it three tremendous knocks, and then ran into the far corner of the hall.

"Oh, Lisita, how could you," cried poor dismayed Paula.

Pretty soon we heard someone coming slowly to the door, but as if he were dragging something behind him with each step, and then the door opened noiselessly, and there stood a forlorn twisted little figure, a lad of about ten years. As we looked at his face with its halo of golden hair we forgot all about his deformities.

"Have you come to see my sister?" he said.

"Yes," said Paula, "that is, we have come to see Mademoiselle Virtud."

"She is very, very sick," he said, and we saw that it was with difficulty that he restrained his tears. As he opened the door a bit wider to let us in, we saw that a black shawl had been placed over the only window in the room, so that it was extremely difficult to see anything in the room.

"Elena," called the boy softly; "here are some visitors to see you."

"For me?" said a voice in the darkness—a voice we recognized at once.

"Well, then, Gabriel, please take the shawl from the window; they will find it too dark here."

"But Elena, the light will make your head ache."

"No, no, dear; it's alright now I've slept a bit, and I feel better."

Presently the shawl came down from the window, allowing us to see the form of poor Mlle. Virtud on the bed.

"Oh," she said, "so it's you! It's very kind of you, dear children, to come and see me!"

We stood near the door transfixed as we looked on the face of our poor sick teacher and we saw what a terrible change a few days had made. The little boy came and stood near his elder sister with a mixed air of concern and deep affection.

"And how is everybody at the school?" asked the invalid. And Paula told her a bit about the small happenings in the class.

"And so Mademoiselle Virginia has taken the class. I am sure you must love her very much."

"Not as much as we do you, dear teacher," said Paula.

"Oh, Paula, you just say that to make me feel good; do you not?" and poor Mlle. Virtud looked from one to the other of us a bit sadly I thought.

At this, Paula came over to the bed and placed her warm hand on the thin cheek of the sick one, as she said, "No, Mademoiselle; it is because it is true, that I said it. You are our dear teacher, and we know that you have sacrificed so much and worked so hard to give us knowledge, and so that is why we love you."

"I did my fifty lines!" I burst out, "that is to say, Paula did twenty-five, and I did the rest."

"What's that you say?" and a smile of amusement passed over the thin features of the teacher, and yet a certain tender look came into her eyes as she said, "You poor little thing! I'd forgotten all about it!"

"Gabriel," she said, turning to the boy who had been examining us minutely, "these are the young ladies who have been sending you such beautiful flowers. You see, he loves flowers so!" explained Mademoiselle. "Poor child, he cannot walk, and so he has to stay here in this stuffy room all day long. Before I was ill, I was able to take him out in his little carriage, and sometimes we would go as far as the open fields where he could see all the flowers he wanted to, to his heart's desire, but now that I'm confined to my bed with this heart-attack, those little excursions have become impossible."

"Are you very sick, Mademoiselle?" Paula asked.

"Oh, I feel much better today. I have suffered greatly. I must get better quickly. Madame Boudre, the principal, wrote me yesterday that she hoped I would be back very soon in my place in the class. Madame Boudre doesn't care to have sick people," and our teacher looked toward the window with its little white curtains and sighed deeply. Gabriel came near the bed, "Don't worry about that, sister; when I get big I will work for you and become rich, and then you won't need to go to school at all."

How many things I was discovering, I who thought that the life of the school-teacher was a bed of roses.

"No, never more," continued the little boy, "I know why you're sick. It's because the school-children trouble you, and as you told me it gave you so much pain to punish them, but when I get big you shall see, as I said before."

Mlle. Virtud looked at the little face with its great earnest eyes.

"I'm afraid you will have to wait a long, long time." she said tenderly, "I don't think I ever told you young ladies that I had a little brother at home. He is the youngest of our family, and I am the oldest."

"How is it that Gabriel is not at home with his parents?" questioned Paula.

"Because, you see, he needed certain special treatments which my parents could not give him in the small village where we live; but here in Rouen there are fine doctors and big hospitals. Of course, I doubt if he can be restored completely, but we are doing all we can. That is my one consolation. I didn't expect that he would be with me so long a time. The first time Gabriel came to Rouen, he went to the big hospital '*Hotel-de-Dieu*' but, after staying there for many months, his hip seemed to be no better, and they could not keep him any longer and then he stayed with me here so that I could take him to the doctor once in a while."

"You'll tire yourself, Mademoiselle, talking to us," broke in Paula, who had learned this much, taking care of Catalina.

"Do you think so," said Mademoiselle, "I know I'm not very well yet, but it isn't very often that I have the pleasure of a visit from my pupils, and so I'm profiting by it. You see, I took Gabriel home once, but when I started to return, the poor boy begged so hard to come back with me that finally my parents agreed; so he's been with me now for several years. We are very happy, are we not, Gabriel? You see, when I'm in school he's able to tidy up the house and wash the dishes. What would I do without my little Gabriel?" she said, as she playfully pulled the little boy's hair.

"And I," said Gabriel, "What would I do without you? In fact, what would everybody do around this whole court without you? Wasn't it you who..."

"There, that will do," said Mlle. Virtud. "You mustn't tell all the family secrets. We are here in this world to help others, are we not, Lisita?"

"Yes, Mademoiselle," I answered, and I was filled with a fear that there might be another sermon coming. However, Mlle. Virtud began to tell us of the rest of the family and of the little village to which they returned at vacation time; and one could see that her heart was there with her loved ones. During the next few minutes there was quite a silence, and I began to shiver with cold, and we noticed that there was no fire in the grate.

"How pale you are," said Mademoiselle; "Are you cold?"

"Yes, a little, Mademoiselle," I said, quite ashamed for my discomfort to be discovered.

"Poor little girl," she said. Taking my two hands in her two hot ones that were burning with fever, "You had better not stay here any longer as you are not accustomed to the cold. Our neighbor made a little fire in the grate this morning to cook the breakfast with, but it's gone out."

Was it this little touch of tenderness on the part of Mademoiselle, or remorse for all the wicked feelings I had so long held against my teacher? Anyway, a flood of tears came as I kneeled beside the bed and hid my face on the white cover. "Oh, Mademoiselle . . . forgive me," I murmured between the sobs.

All my pride had broken and I saw myself for what I was, guilty, unjust and cruel toward this young woman whom I had accused of living solely for herself. I felt a hand passing slowly over my head.

"I forgive you with all my heart, poor child," and the invalid's voice was both sincere and kindly, and I rose and embraced her with a repentant heart, and with a hearty kiss I buried our old war then and there, and in that cold room I felt the warmth of the beginning of a new life for me although at that time I could not have analyzed it. Suddenly we heard a knock on the door.

"Ah, that will be Madame Bertin," said Gabriel, as he hitched himself to the door and opened it, revealing a gray-haired woman who came in on tiptoe.

"Ah, you have visitors, Mademoiselle," as she stopped a moment near the door.

"Only two of my pupils who have come to see me. Come in, come in, it's all right," insisted our teacher.

"Ah," said the new arrival with great interest, "so you are my Victoria's schoolmates. How proud you ought to be to have such a wonderful teacher!" Here she advanced to the bed. "Well, I declare," she said, "you have no more drinking water!" She shook a flask near the bedside saying, "I will go and fill it and bring back a little something to make a fire with so as to get your tea ready. I'm sure Gabriel must be hungry by this time," and without waiting for a reply the good woman went rapidly down the four flights of stairs. Paula then gave Mademoiselle the small package Teresa had sent, as well as the little bag of oranges.

"See, Gabriel!" said Mademoiselle as she opened the packages with delight, "Oranges—and chocolate! What a treat! You are very good to remember me in such a lovely way. Please thank your Teresa, too."

"She said she was coming to see you," said Paula.

At this the poor woman looked disturbed. "I'm afraid she'll find things in a very bad state here," and she colored slightly.

But as we started to go away Paula assured her that Teresa wouldn't mind a bit.

"Just a moment," said the invalid; "Would you mind reading me a chapter out of this book? I have not been able to read it today, as my head ached too badly. It's a book that I love very much."

"The Bible!" cried Paula, "Oh, I didn't know that you read it too."

The young lady shook her head sadly, "I used to read it when I was a child, Paula. It was and is the beloved Book of my mother, but for many, many years I never opened it. When your uncle came to inscribe you as a pupil, he told me how much you loved your father's Bible, and that started me thinking of my own, hidden at the bottom of my trunk, and so I began to read many chapters that I remember having read with my mother, and now I believe that Gabriel would never tire if I read it to him all day."

"Tell her to read the story of Jesus healing the sick people," came the eager voice of Gabriel.

Mademoiselle smiled, "Gabriel's right. When people are sick they love to hear of the greatest doctor of all. Read about the ten lepers, Paula."

At this point the old lady returned, and she too stood and listened as Paula began to read the wonderful story.

"And as Jesus came to Jerusalem, He went through Galilee, and entering into a village, behold ten lepers stood afar off, and cried, Jesus, Master, have mercy on us, and He said to them, Go show yourselves to the priest. And as they went their way, they were healed, and one of them seeing that he was healed, returned and glorified God in a loud voice, and cast himself at the feet of Jesus, giving thanks to Him, and behold, he was a Samaritan. Then said Jesus, Were there not ten healed? Where are the nine? Only this foreigner has returned to give glory to God. And He said to him, Rise, therefore; thy faith hath made thee whole" (Luke 17:11-19). Here Paula stopped, not knowing whether to go on to the end of the chapter.

Mlle. Virtud then closed her eyes, but one could see she was not sleeping. Paula waited in silence, and so did the old lady as she stood there with her rough, toil-worn hands clasped beneath her apron.

"Read some more," said Gabriel, "No," said Mlle. Virtud. "It's time the children returned, for they must reach home before dark." She drew us to her, giving us both a long embrace. "May God bless you both, my dear young friends! Come back soon to see me." Then Victoria's mother embraced us also, saying the same time, "I have a poor blind daughter. I would be very grateful if you would stop in to see her the next time and read her the same story you have just read to Mademoiselle."

"I don't know how to read," she continued; "I have such a poor stupid head, and Victoria doesn't seem to have learned to read very well. She can show you where we live,—and now, goodbye until next time."

On our return Teresa prepared supper. She was more hurried than usual because she had to get the week's wash ready for the next day; but she listened with great interest, nevertheless, to the story of our afternoon's visit. "I'm going to see her tomorrow, poor child," she said.

That night Teresa came to tuck us in and kiss us goodnight which was her habit, as she said, to try to take partly the place of our poor dear mother. I whispered in her ear, "Teresa, I've come to love Mademoiselle Virtud."

"Good! Good!" exclaimed the old servant; "that's something new indeed! And why has the wind so suddenly changed in her direction?"

"It's because I know her now!" I said.

Teresa seated herself on my bed, and in spite of the cold she talked to me a long time, telling me that my heart's coldness and my selfishness had caused her much grief. I could see how happy I had made her to have confessed my faults and thus show the beginning of a great change. She told me how my mother died with a prayer on her lips for me. Then she spoke of Paula who thought of nothing except making other people happy. "Wouldn't you like to be like Paula?" Teresa questioned me. "Of course, dear Teresa," I said, "but that's impossible, I'm too bad for that."

"Who it is, Lisita, that makes Paula so good?" and Teresa's voice took on a new and most tender note.

"It's the Lord Jesus!" I answered in a low whisper.

"That's well answered, Lisita! And the same Lord Jesus would do the like for you. Let me ask you something. Do you not find me changed—since,—since,—I began to pray to Him?"

"Yes, Teresa."

"In what way have you noticed the change?"

"Well, for one thing—wash-day doesn't make you irritable, as it used to do," I said.

"That's something, now isn't it? Oh, when one has the peace of God in the heart, anger doesn't have a chance to get inside as it used to do."

I looked at her furtively. By the lamplight I could see in those dark blue eyes such a new, such a tender, confident look, that in spite of the wrinkled cheeks and her white hair I saw a startling likeness to Paula herself. I couldn't explain it at the time, but later I understood—Teresa and Paula were just part of the family of God and it was His likeness of Jesus, His dear Son, I had seen in both of them.

PART TWO

Chapter One

SOME YEARS LATER

The years passed swiftly without bringing any great changes in our quiet life. Our grandparents had aged a bit, and Teresa was not quite as active as formerly, while a few wrinkles had gathered on our father's forehead; but all this had come so slowly that the change was hardly noticed.

Rosa, who was now eighteen years old, was studying in the city. She was still the same—studious, faithful and sincere in all that she did. Her quiet reserved manner caused some people to call her proud, but those who knew her better loved her, and knew she could be depended on in time of trouble.

Catalina still suffered somewhat, but now was able to walk around a bit without crutches, and in spite of her delicate health and poor twisted body she had come bravely to take her true place among us as our "big sister," so loving and solicitous for everybody's welfare that she came to be known in the neighborhood as "The little mother."

Paula was now fourteen years of age. In the house, at school, in the village, everywhere, everybody loved her, and I can say with all honesty that never a shadow of envy ever disturbed the tender friendship, which had united us to her from the beginning. One could not possibly be jealous of Paula. All that she possessed was ours. Our joys were hers. Our sorrows were her sorrows. She had grown in body and mind, and yet had kept the same characteristics. Always bright and happy and full of fun, she had the same simple, humble ways as when at ten years of age she had come among

135

us. Her special summer delight was to run through the fields, always returning to the house with a big bunch of wild flowers for Catalina. In one thing only she always seemed to fail. Teresa had a fearful task in teaching her to sew and to knit.

"What are you going to do in the future if you don't know how to do these things?"

"I'm sure I don't know," Paula would say sadly, and would take up the work once more with such sweet resignation that Teresa, moved with compassion, would take the work from her hands saying—"There! There! Run outdoors now for a bit of fresh   air."

Then away Paula would go into the garden or under the trees that lined the village street. Soon she was back with such a happy smile that Teresa forgave her completely.

Once however Teresa lost all patience with her, exclaiming, as she saw the strange ragged ends she had left in her sewing, "Drop that work, and go where you please; but remember this, never will you be called a 'Dorcas.' Never will you be able to sew and provide garments for the poor. It's not enough to tell them you love them, you must show it by your works—and the best way to do that would be to learn to be useful to them."

Paula sat back stiff and straight in consternation. "Oh, Teresa, I never, never thought of that!" she said in a tone of greatest remorse, "Oh, please let me go on! I will try to do better!"

But Teresa had taken away the work, and was not inclined to be easily persuaded. "No, not now! Another time perhaps you may show what you can do."

Paula therefore had to submit; but that was the last time that Teresa had any reason to complain. That afternoon Paula had gone straight to her room, and I followed soon after to comfort her, but I found her kneeling by her bedside pouring her heart in true repentance to Him who was ever her unseen Companion. I closed the door gently behind me and stole away.

Later Paula said to me, "Oh, Lisita, I'm surely bad indeed. One thing I've certainly hated to do, and that is to sit down and learn to sew, especially in fine weather like this. I seem to hear a thousand voices that call me out-of-doors. I never could see any earthly reason why I should have to learn how to sew, and so I never even tried to please Teresa in that way. But now she tells me that if I go on like this I shall never be able to sew for the poor. I never thought of that! I wonder what the Lord Jesus must think of me. He gave His life for me, and here I am not willing to learn something that would help me to put clothes on poor folks! Oh, I must! I must learn to sew, no matter what it costs."

That was it—to do something for others, that was the principal thing in all her thoughts.

In school Paula never did win prizes—nor did I. Both of us were generally about on an equal level at the bottom of our class.

About a year after our first visit to Mademoiselle Virtud's house, Madame Boudre had moved us up to the Third Grade. Teresa made a magnificent apple-cake as a sign of her pleasure. My father also showed his great satisfaction, and in fact everybody rejoiced to see that at last we were both making progress. In spite of all, however, there was one great heavy weight on my heart, and I cried myself to sleep that night. I think Mlle. Virtud also felt badly that we were leaving her, but she made us promise to come and visit her. "You are no longer my pupils," she said, "but you are still, and will be always, my dear friends."

Gabriel was so glad to see us that it was always a joy to go and play with him on our Thursday half-holidays. Paula always told him Bible stories, for that seemed to be his chief pleasure, and I taught him to read. Victoria's mother used to bring her work over to Mlle. Virtud's room and heard the stories with great delight.

"If I had been able to leave my Victoria in school she would have become as wise and learned as you, Mesdemoiselles," she would say a bit sadly at times. "But there, I can't complain; what would we have done without the money she earns at the factory?"

One afternoon we said good-bye to Gabriel and mounted the stairs to visit the blind girl. Left alone for most of the day, she passed the long hours knitting. She was about the same age as our Catalina, but she appeared to be much older. The first time we had visited her, she had hardly raised her head from her work, and showed but little interest in the stories that her mother had asked us to read to her. It was not so much indifference as an apparent incapacity to comprehend the meaning of what she heard. But on this particular afternoon Paula started singing a hymn. The poor girl suddenly dropped her work in her lap, and listened with rapt attention. When Paula had finished she exclaimed "Oh, mamma! Mamma! Tell her to please sing again!"

Mme. Bertin could not suppress the cry of delight as she said, "Dear Mademoiselle Paula, please sing another song! Never have I seen Marguerite so happy." And so Paula sang hymn after hymn. As Paula at last stopped singing, for the time had come to go home, poor Marguerite stretched out her arms as if groping for something.

"Please do not be offended, Mademoiselle Paula," implored Madame Bertin; "she wants you to come nearer that she may feel your face. The blind have no other eyes." Paula kneeled at Marguerite's side and the blind girl passed her hands gently over the upturned face, pausing an instant at the broad forehead, then on over the beautiful arched brows and long eyelashes and the delicately-fashioned nose and lips, that smiled softly as she touched them.

"You have not seen her hair," said the mother, as she guided the girl's hands upward and over the waves of light brown hair that seemed like an aurora fit for such a face, and then finally down the long braids that extended below Paula's waist. Then with one of those sudden movements characteristic of the blind, she carried the shining braids to her lips and kissed them as in ecstasy. Then, just as suddenly, in confusion dropped them and buried her own face in her hands.

At this Paula sprang to her feet and put her arms about the poor girl, and murmured in her ear, "We do love you so, Marguerite!"

After that visit, little by little Marguerite began to love to hear us speak of the Saviour. Her indifference and sadness disappeared, giving place to a quiet peace and joy that was contagious for all who came in contact with her. Mme. Bertin no longer called her "My poor daughter," only "My Marguerite." For the next two years she became our constant delight. Teresa at times gave us clothes but slightly worn to take to her, which gave us almost as much joy as we carried them to Marguerite as she herself felt on receiving them.

One day Gabriel came running to tell us that Marguerite was quite ill, and we lost no time in going to see her. With painful feelings of presentiment we mounted the steep stairs to her room.

As we entered, Madame Bertin came toward us with her apron to her eyes and Mlle. Virtud made signs for us to come over to the bed, as she slightly raised the sick girl's head.

"Dearest Marguerite," said our teacher; "Here are Paula and Lisita."

"May God bless them both," and Marguerite spread out her arms toward us, adding, "Oh, Paula, please sing again, 'There's No Night There!'" And Paula sang once more the old hymns.

"In the land of fadeless day
Lies the city foursquare;
It shall never pass away,
And there is no night there.

God shall wipe away all tears;
There's no death, no pain, nor fears;
And they count not time by years,
For there is no night there."

"Oh, how beautiful!" And it seemed as if the poor blind girl were straining those sightless orbs for a glimpse of the Beautiful City. "Don't cry, mother," she said as she caught a low sob form the other end of the room. "I am so happy now to go to be with Jesus." The poor mother put her face close to her daughter's lips so that she might not lose a word.

"One regret only I have, Mamma," Marguerite said; "and that is, that I have never seen your face. Oh, that I might have seen it just once."

"In Heaven," interrupted our teacher, "you eyes will be open forever."

"Oh, yes," said the dying girl. "There perhaps I will see Mamma and Victoria. Will you please give Victoria a kiss for me when she comes home from the factory tonight. Tell her I'm so grateful; she has worked so hard for us!" Then suddenly—"Paula!" she called,—"Paula!"

"Here I am, Marguerite," and Paula came closer, taking her hand.

"Ah, you are here. Thanks, dear Paula," she gasped. "Many thanks for telling me about Jesus and His love for me. Sing"—The sentence was never finished, but Paula's sweet voice rose, as once again she sang the sublime words:

"There is no night there."

"Is she dead?" I said, as we looked down on the still white face.

"Yes, but soon her eyes shall be open," said Mlle. Virtud tenderly, "in the city where there is no night!"

Chapter Two

THE BRETON

It was a snowy, blustery day. It is always a source of pleasure to see the drifts beginning to bank against the houses across the street. On this afternoon the bushes and roofs were already crowned in white, and all the trees were festooned as if for a holiday. The smaller objects in the garden had disappeared under this grand upholstery of nature, and the rattle of the carts and other ordinary sounds of the village were muffled in the mantle of snow. To be sure Paula dampened my pleasure a bit by reminding me that there were many people who were in great suffering on account of the storm, without proper food, warm clothing, or fire in their houses.

It had been a hard winter. Many of the factories in town had had to discharge their workers on account of lack of orders. Happily, Teresa with Catalina's help had done all she could to aid the poor folks in our neighborhood. Paula had sewed incessantly. Her stitches were pretty uneven and the thread frequently knotted in her nervous hands, but Teresa said that the mistakes she made were more than made up by the love that she put into her work.

I read to Paula while she sewed, and we were certainly happy when at last the mountain of old clothes which had been gathered for the poor had been made over and finally distributed to the needy ones.

I remember especially one poor woman to whom Teresa had sent us with a package of clothes, who received us with tears of gratitude.

And now, as I sat looking out at the gathering drifts, I heard Catalina remark in a relieved tone, "At last *that's* finished!"

"What's finished?" I asked. "My old dress," she said. "Who would have thought I could do a job like this! But there it is turned and darned and lengthened. Happily, I don't believe that poor Celestina Dubois will be very difficult to please"—And Catalina pulled a comical smile.

As one looked at that peaceful beautiful face it was hard to realize that it could belong to the poor miserable invalid of a short time before!

"What a shame that it's still snowing so hard," she said, "I would have liked to have sent it over to Celestina today. Teresa says the poor woman needs it badly. But I suppose we'll have to wait till morning."

"That won't be at all necessary," said Paula, "We're not afraid of a little snow, are we, Lisita? If you only knew how I love to go out into a snowstorm like this!"

"You must be like the mountain goats of your own country," said Catalina with a laugh. "To think of getting any pleasure in going out in a snowstorm!"

"Oh, no!" said Paula. "The goats don't like the cold."

"Well, I declare!" said Catalina, "I wouldn't have believed that! Well, run and ask permission of Teresa."

And Teresa dressed us up as if we were going on a voyage to the North Pole and gave us a thousand instructions. "Above all things don't 'dilly-dally' on the way," she said. "The Breton was released from jail today, and you may depend on it he will not be in a very good humor. What a shame that Celestina should have such a terrible neighbor. You can never tell what a man like that may do. If my rheumatism would only let me, I would gladly go with you."

"What on earth would we do if we happened to meet the Breton?" I questioned Paula, and terror began to grip my heart as we drew near the drunkard's house.

"Don't you be afraid, Lisita," said Paula, taking my trembling hand in hers.

Celestina received us with exclamations of surprise and delight.

Overcome with emotion, she said, "To think of your coming to see me through all this terrible storm! I never would have expected you on such a day!"

We noticed a shade of sadness in her tone, and Paula questioned her as to the reason.

The old lady shook her head. "No, there's nothing particular," she said; "the Lord seems to heap good things upon me; but at times on nearing the end of the journey the pilgrim gets a bit tired and longs for the blessed final rest." Then she paused and turned to us once more with a smile. "And you, young people, how goes the journey with you?"

"I too find," said Paula gravely, "that at times the way is difficult, but as we put our hand in that of the Lord Jesus, He helps and strengthens us."

The old lady's eyes were full of amusement as she answered, "My, oh, me! You talk as wisely as an old traveler who is about to finish his long journey instead of being still at the bottom of the hill. And your uncle! Has he began to go with you yet?" "My uncle," and Paula hesitated, "at least he permits us to serve the Lord."

"But he doesn't let you attend church yet?"

"No, but I think he will some day."

"Courage, Paula," said the old woman, "The Lord Jesus has said, 'Be thou faithful unto death, and I will give thee the crown of life!' How happy I shall be when your uncle permits you to attend with us. I know the Lord has saved you and given you eternal life, and He will do exceeding abundantly above all you can ask or think. I've learned to say to Him, 'Thy will be done!' While here on this earth we're all students in His school. Sometimes the hours are long and the bench is hard, but if we are attentive and apt in the learning of our lessons, He is faithful, and oh, so generous in giving us of His good things! Some things He's tried to teach me, but I'm too dull yet to comprehend, but I do know that some day He'll let me see it all quite clearly. For example, it's difficult to understand why He should have given me the Breton and his children for neighbors. Do you know the family?" she asked us.

"Oh, yes, indeed," said I; "I should say we did." This long conversation had made me sleepy, but the mention of the Breton had brought me wide-awake again.

"If I had known," continued the old lady, "that on the other side of the partition I was to hear nothing but quarrels and fighting and cursing, I would never have moved here, but more that that, not content with disturbing the peace from within his own apartment, he even comes over to my side to torment me here in my small room. The Breton indeed is a terrible man when he's drunk. I have tried to talk to him to see if I could do something to change his evil ways, but so far all my efforts have been useless."

I interrupted her to ask if she knew he had been liberated from the jail that very day.

"Oh, yes," she said; "he made a terrible scene this morning bullying his poor wife around. The poor soul is certainly worthy of our pity. But here I am talking on and on without enquiring once as to Catalina's health."

"It was Catalina herself who sent us with this package for you," said Paula. "For me!" cried the old lady. "What's all this?" and she nervously untied the strings. Then as she saw the warm dress, her eyes filled with tears. "May the Lord bless the dear girl! He surely must have revealed to her my need!"

"Would you mind, please, putting it on? Catalina wanted us to find out if it fits you," I said.

The good woman nothing loath tried on the dress as she exclaimed, "My, oh, me, how handsome I am for once in my life, at least," and a merry twinkle danced in Celestina's eyes, "I'll have to keep this for Sunday wear only."

"No," said Paula, "Catalina said to be sure to tell you it was for everyday wear, for you see how it keeps out the cold."

"Well, then," said the old lady, "I suppose I must obey orders. But my, how beautiful it is, too beautiful for the likes of me!" And Celestina stroked the lovely cloth with her gnarled and withered fingers. "How very good the dear Lord is! And now if you don't mind, let us pray together to thank Him for all His mercies." Celestina who could not kneel, placed her hands on our bowed heads, and after a heartfelt prayer of thanks asked the Lord to bless us each one and each member of our family, her neighbors, and lastly herself.

Hardly had she finished when uncertain steps were heard coming down the passage. The door suddenly burst open and a man staggered into the room.

"What's this you're doing?" he shouted.

"We're praying," the old woman answered tranquilly.

"No more praying then! Do you hear me? I forbid you!" he shouted again in such a terrible voice that it was all I could do to keep from screaming with fright.

"You know very well," said Celestina calmly, "that you cannot prohibit my doing the thing that pleases me in my own house."

"And what pleasure do you get out of praying, tell me, you pious old hypocrite!"

"Well, if you'll sit down calmly in that chair yonder, I'll answer your questions."

"And suppose I don't care to sit down! Do I look as if I were tired?"

"Perhaps not, but when you visit your friends you should try to please them, shouldn't you?"

"What! Do you count me as one of your friends?"

"And why not?"

"This is why!" and the Breton shook his great fist in the old lady's face. "Oh, I'm a bad one I am! I could kill all three of you in a jiffy! Why, I just finished a month in the jail for 'regulating' a fellow-worker at the factory, and I don't mind doing another month for regulating you people!" And the poor fellow's face was more terrible than his words, and I thought our "time had come," as the saying is.

"Now, don't you be afraid," whispered Celestina, as she drew me close; "God is with us; don't forget that!"

"Why do you wish to harm us?" she said aloud, fixing her eyes on the poor drunken brute, in such a calm, loving and compassionate way that it seemed to calm him a bit. "We've done nothing against you, and I can't for the life of me see how we could have offended you. I am glad they let you go free. Now if you care to accept our hospitality I will make you a cup of coffee. It's not the best quality but you're welcome to what I have."

The Breton looked at the old lady in an astonished sort of way. "You're certainly different from the rest of 'em. Here I threaten to kill you, and you offer me a cup of coffee! That's not what I deserve," and here he broke out laughing immoderately, and sat down by the stove where a fire was briskly burning.

"Well, this is a whole lot better than the prison anyway," said the Breton coolly, as he settled himself to enjoy the warmth.

"I should say so," said Celestina, "and there's no reason for you to go back there either."

"Now none of your sermons, you know, for if you come on with anything like that I'll be leaving at once," and it was clear that the Breton's bad humor was returning.

"Well, that would be to your disadvantage on a cold day like this," said Celestina with a dry little smile.

"That's a fact, that's a fact. Brr! What weather!" and the poor drunkard drew closer to the fire. "Aren't you two afraid to go out in such a snowstorm?" he said, turning to Paula and me.

Celestina answered for us that we lived in the big house at "The Convent," and that we had come to deliver a good warm dress for her to wear. With that the good woman poured out three cups of coffee, which she set before the Breton, Paula and myself. "And where's yours?" said the Breton as he swallowed his coffee in one giant gulp.

"Oh, some other time I'll have a cup myself."

"Well, just as you please," said our unwelcome guest. "My! But that warms one up though! My wife never so much as thought to get me a cup of coffee."

"And do you know why?" questioned Celestina severely.

"I suppose you're going to tell me it's because I don't give her enough money; is that it?"

"Precisely! And that's the truth; isn't it?"

"Now none of your sermons, as I told you in the beginning; didn't I? Don't I know? Of course it troubles me to see the children with their pale faces, that used to be rosy and fat like these two here. By the way what's your names?"

Again Celestina answered for us—"The smaller girl is the daughter of Monsieur Dumas, and the other is her cousin, Mademoiselle Paula Javanel."

"Paula Javanel! Paula Javanel!" repeated the Breton as if trying to remember something. "I think I've heard that name before," and he looked fixedly at Paula for some seconds, and then suddenly laughed immoderately. "Yes, yes; now I remember! Ha! Ha! Ha! Now I know! You're the 'Cat Mother'!"

"Cat Mother!" and Celestina looked much puzzled. "What on earth do you mean?" I had completely forgotten the ridiculous nickname that the Breton's son had given her, for the boy had run away from home several years ago.

"They called me that," explained Paula, "because I once saved a cat's life."

But the strong coffee had quite restored the Breton's good humor and he hastened to add, "Yes, she did; but she hasn't told the whole story! She's the only person in the whole village that was brave enough to stand up to that big brat of mine. She wrenched the cat out of his hands, and the boy came back to the house, I remember well, with a pair of ears well pulled and the air of a whipped dog."

"But I didn't pull his ears," said Paula, reddening.

"Well, if you didn't, who did, then?"

But Paula shook her head and would say nothing further.

"Well, anyway, I remember that the boy was made fun of by the whole neighborhood, and to revenge himself he gave her 'Cat Mother' for a nickname. He, too, is a bad one like his father. To tell the truth he never obeyed anybody, and dear knows where he is or what he's doing now. At least he's not like you two who come here to learn how to pray with Celestina."

"Paula doesn't need to learn how to pray, Monsieur Breton," said Celestina, "she's known how to pray for years, not only for herself, but also for others."

"For years, you say! And who then taught her to pray?" said the Breton surprised.

"It was my father," said Paula quietly.

"Your father! Well, he wasn't much like me, then; was he!"

"No, he wasn't," and Paula without sign of either fear or abhorrence looked compassionately at the brutalized face that confronted her.

"And you don't live with him anymore?"

"No," said Paula; "father is dead."

"And whatever would you do if you had a father like me?" and the poor Breton looked at her keenly.

Paula sat a moment with closed eyes. She recalled the strong noble face and figure of her dear father and asked God to give her a reply to the poor drunkard's question.

"I think," she said at last, "I would ask God Himself to make him a man of God like my father."

"And do you believe He could do it?" The Breton looked very doubtful.

"I'm sure of it!"

"Yes, but you don't know how bad I am."

'Yes, I know," said Paula; "everybody in town knows you're a bad man, but you're no worse than the bandit who was crucified, with the Lord Jesus; and yet Christ saved him; didn't He?"

"That's more or less what I am—a bandit, I suppose. I remember the story. When I was a little boy my mother told it to me. I never thought at that time that I'd ever become the thing I am today. What would my poor mother do if she could see what had become of me?"

"Perhaps she'd pray for you," Paula said simply.

"She! Yes, I think she would have prayed for me," he said. "But why talk about my mother! I, who have just come out of prison—hated, despised, and made a laughing-stock by everybody in our neighborhood, even pointed at by the little street-urchins! My children fear me! My poor wife trembles when I appear! Who would ever think of praying for a brute like me?"

"I," said Paula with a voice vibrant with emotion.

"You? Why you scarcely know me!"

"But I do know you, and I've prayed many times for you, Monsieur Breton. Do you think it didn't distress me when they told me you had been put in the prison where people say it's so cold and dark inside, and where many die from exposure, and what is the greater calamity—die without hope of salvation."

"And so, while I was in prison you prayed for me?"

"Well, from the time I heard about it," said Paula, "I've prayed for you every night, Monsieur Breton."

The poor fellow bowed his head. This young girl, so beautiful, so pure, so innocent, had taken him and his shame, and misery and wickedness, to the throne of Grace in her prayers each night during his recent stay in the jail!

"You! You've been praying for me!" The Breton remained silent, overcome with a greater remorse than he had ever felt in a court of justice.

"If I could believe," he said in a low voice, "that a man like me could really change—but no! That's impossible! It's too late!"

"It's not too late," Celestina said, "God pardons sinners always if they truly repent. Now you listen to what he says: 'Though your sins be as scarlet, they shall be as white as snow; though they be red like crimson, they shall be as wool.' And here's a bit more, 'Seek ye the Lord while He may be found, call ye upon Him while He is near; let the wicked forsake his way and the unrighteous man his thoughts; and let him return unto the Lord, and He will have mercy upon him;

and to our God for He will abundantly pardon.' And then St. Paul gives us God's message also with these words:

"For this is good and acceptable in the sight of God our Saviour; who will have all men to be saved, and to come unto the knowledge of the truth. For there is one God, and one Mediator between God and men, the Man Christ Jesus; who gave Himself a ransom for all" (1 Timothy 2:3-6).

"Do you really believe," said the Breton, as if in a daze, "that there's hope for such as me?"

"Yes, I do, indeed!" And here Celestina quoted,

"The Lord is longsuffering to us-ward, not willing that any should perish, but that all should come to repentance" (2 Peter 3:9).

But the poor Breton shook his head as if to say, "It's impossible!"

Here Paula broke in, "Ask pardon now, and Jesus will pardon you! Ask it now! Surely you don't want to go on as you have done. The Lord loves you, and is waiting to save you. He shed His blood on Calvary's cross to take away the guilt of your sin. Then also, would it not be wonderful to always have bread in the house—to see that your poor wife no longer fears you, but instead welcomes your homecoming. Ask Him now, Monsieur Breton, and He'll work the miracle in you just as He did when He made the paralyzed man to walk. You would be so much happier than you are now."

She had drawn very close to him, and now she took his great gnarled hands—those hands that so many times had worn the handcuffs. Taking them in her own beautiful ones, she raised those wonderful eyes to the brutal, bloated face, and said simply, "We will help you, Monsieur Breton!"

"And what are you going to do, Mademoiselle?"

"I don't know yet, but we'll do what we can!"

The poor fellow tried to thank her, but could not utter a word. Something in his throat seemed to be in the way, and in spite of all his efforts at self-control, great tears began to run down his cheeks.

Suddenly he turned exclaiming, "Let me alone! Don't you see you're tearing my very heart out! For thirty long years I've never shed a tear."

Here Celestina quoted Isaiah 35:8, 9, 10: "And a highway shall be there, and a Way; and it shall be called the Way of Holiness; the unclean shall not pass over it, but it shall be for those: the wayfaring men, though fools, shall not err therein. No lion shall be there, nor any ravenous beast shall go up thereon, it shall not be found there; but the redeemed shall walk there: and the ransomed of the Lord shall return, and come to Zion with songs and everlasting joy upon their heads: they shall obtain joy and gladness, and sorrow and sighing shall flee away."

But the Breton had turned the door-handle.

"You're surely not going out yet!" said the old lady sadly.

"Celestina, I must go! If I stay one minute more I know I must yield, and I'm not going to do anything foolish. No! No! I've served the devil too long. But look here! If you wish to help me, then you can do one thing anyway. You can pray for me!" Saying this, the poor Breton opened the door and was gone.

Chapter Three

SAVED!

That night on our return we poured into Teresa's sympathetic ears all that had occurred during our eventful visit that afternoon at Celestina's house. Then somewhat later as I was helping her with the dishes in the kitchen, Teresa said, "Do you know, Lisita, it wouldn't surprise me in the least to see the Breton converted and changed by God's power into a decent, respectable man. No one seems to be able to resist Paula when she begins to speak of God's love. She seems truly inspired by His Holy Spirit. Child though she is, she surely is His messenger to all with whom she comes in contact. But there's just one thing,"—and Teresa seemed to hesitate to express herself, then finally she continued, "I cannot seem to shake off the feeling that she will not be with us much longer. I believe somehow,—I know it sounds absurd in one way, but I have a feeling that God will call her to His side some day soon."

"Oh, Teresa!" I cried, "how can you say such a thing! Why, she's never sick! She's much bigger and stronger and more vigorous than even I am. And besides, I never, never could bear it to have Paula taken away from me!"

"Hush! Hush, child! Don't shout that way, Paula will hear you! Besides it's just a foolish idea of mine, maybe. But if God should wish it—But there, as you say, what would we do without the dear girl?"

Later when we were alone in our bedroom I said to Paula in an anxious tone,

"You don't feel sick; do you Paula?"

154

She looked at me surprised—"I should say not!" She laughed, "What put such a notion in your head? Do I look as if I was sick?"

I was so relieved! Teresa was quite mistaken!

"No!" continued Paula, "on the contrary, I never felt better in my life. Since I had that little touch of scarletina a while ago I've never had an ache or pain. In fact, as I look around and see so much sickness and suffering, I long to share my good health with these other less fortunate ones."

And as I looked at her tall well-developed figure outlined against the window, I laughed at my foolish fears. But a few moments later as she kneeled there in the moonlight in her long white dress, and as I looked at that pure beautiful face with the eyes closed in prayer, with its frame of glorious hair, I knew that never had I seen anything so lonely as this child companion of mine just budding into womanhood; and the one word "Angel" seemed to express the sum of my thoughts regarding this dear one who had come into my life and who had transformed so many other lives around me.

As she rose at the conclusion of the prayer, finding me still on my feet, she said with surprise in her tone, "Not in bed yet, Lisita?"

"No," I said, confused that she should find me still seated on the edge of my bed, lost in my own reflections.

Paula suddenly went to the window and looked out, "Oh, Lisita!" she exclaimed, "how wonderful! Come and see."

The storm had stopped in the late afternoon, and now the moon shone in all its splendor, touching the snow with silver and making millions of its crystals sparkle like diamonds in the moonlight.

"How white and pure and beautiful everything is!" said Paula. "Do you remember, Lisita, how only yesterday we remarked how squalid and dirty the whole village looked?

And now, what a lovely change!" She hesitated a moment, and then continued in her quiet, simple way.

"It's God that has done it! It's quite a bit like when one gives their heart to Jesus Christ. He takes it stained and scarred with sin, and then He makes it white like the snow. Don't you see, Lisita?"

"Yes, I see," I said.

"Do you really see, dear Lisita?" And Paula drew me quite close to her. "Then why don't you give your heart to Him? I do love you so! You see, I don't wish to be any better then you—but when I get thinking of the fact that you never really have given your heart to Him, and if one of us should die—"

I could not bear another word. The very idea of death either for Paula or myself was simply unbearable. "Stop!" I cried, in such a terrible tone that Paula, I could see, was frightened. "You mustn't die! I cannot live, and I *won't* live without you! I know I'm not good, but if you weren't here to help me what would I do?"

My overwrought nerves, due to the happenings at that afternoon visit at Celestina's, combined with what Teresa had suggested, were too much for me, and here I broke down completely.

"Oh, Lisita!"—there was real consternation in Paula's voice, "I'm so sorry I hurt you! You must get to bed, and don't let's talk anymore tonight."

I dreamed of Paula the whole night long. I saw her either dying or dead, or in heaven with the angels; but in the morning all my fears had disappeared and a few days later I even forgot the whole thing.

A week passed, and we had seen nothing of the Breton. Paula mentioned him several times, and I know she was praying for him. Teresa had gone to see Celestina, but she hadn't seen anything of him either. Apparently he had gone out early each day, and had returned very late. He had been the principal subject of our conversation as each night we came together in the big warm kitchen on those long winter evenings. Finally one evening just as we were finishing dishes, there came two hesitating knocks on the outer door.

"I wonder who can be calling at this hour," said Rosa. "It sounds like some child that can't knock very well," said Catalina. "Open the door, Lisita!"

Only too glad to abandon my towel, I ran to open the door, but hardly had I done so when I remained petrified and dumb with surprise, hardly able to believe my own eyes. There stood the Breton twisting his battered cap nervously between his bony fingers. The little oil lamp, which we always kept lighted at night in the passageway, illuminated his pale face and gaunt figure.

"Good evening, mademoiselle," he finally managed to say, and then he stopped, apparently as embarrassed as I was.

"Who it is?" said Teresa, as she started to come to my rescue.

"It's the Breton," I said.

"Well, tell him to come in," said the old woman kindly.

As timidly as a child the Breton advanced over the threshold a few paces, looking about him in a kind of "lost" way until his eyes encountered Paula, and then he seemed to recover his ease of mind.

"I wish to speak with the Master," he said—directing his words to Teresa.

She led him into the study where my father sat, and left them together and then joined us in the kitchen once more.

"I declare!" said Rosa. "Think of the Breton calling on us! I thought he hated father since that day he discharged him from the factory two or three years ago."

"The Breton knows very well that when your father got rid of him he well deserved it," said Teresa, as she adjusted her spectacles and settled down to her knitting.

My father did not keep him long. From the kitchen we could hear the door open and my father's voice bidding the Breton a kindly "good night." Evidently the interview, although short, had been quite a cordial one.

"Go, tell the Breton to come into the kitchen, Lisita," said Teresa.

I wondered as I saw him enter with such a humble, frank air, and with a new look of peace that seemed almost to beautify the brutalized face.

"Mademoiselle Paula," he said as he stopped in the middle of our kitchen, "I wish to say a word or two."

"To me alone?" said Paula rising.

He hesitated a moment. "No," he said finally, "I think it's better to say it to you before everybody here. Do you remember how you spoke to me on the afternoon of the great snow? I don't remember very well what you said. My head wasn't in very good condition as I'd left my wits behind at the liquor shop. But I know you spoke to me of my mother and you also said that God would change me if I really desired. I didn't dare believe such a thing. Mademoiselle—it seemed just a bit too good to believe. That night I simply couldn't sleep. I seemed to feel my hands in yours and to hear your voice saying, 'I'll do what I can to help you.' At last I couldn't stand it any longer. I got out on the floor and kneeled there before God, and asked Him to have mercy on me, and change my wicked old heart if it were possible."

Here he stopped to wipe away the great tears that were rolling down his cheeks. Then pretty soon he continued, "God did indeed have mercy on me. I deserved to be refused, but apparently He doesn't treat people as they deserve to be treated, and now, mademoiselle, will you continue to help me as you promised to do?"

"Yes, of course," said Paula; "What can we do for you?"

"Just one thing. Pray for me! That's what I need more than anything else. I want to be faithful to Him and serve Him, but I don't know how to begin, and when one has served the devil as many years as I have it's hard to change masters."

"The Lord Jesus will help you," answered Paula.

"He's already done it, Mademoiselle," said the Breton. "If not, how could I have endured these last days. At first I had a raging thirst for more drink until I nearly went crazy. Then my old companions called me out and urged me to go and drink with them, and I had almost yielded when suddenly I cried to the Lord Jesus to help me, and then a wonderful thing happened! All desire for the drink went away, and I've been free ever since! Then too, I had no work, and my wife taunted me with that, and I wandered up and down looking everywhere for something to do. Unfortunately everybody knew me and knew too much about me, so there was no work for such as me." Then suddenly the poor thin face was illuminated with a smile as the Breton triumphantly said, "I came to this door tonight as the very last resort, never dreaming that my old master really would employ me, but just see the goodness of God! I can face the world again, for I'm going back to my old bench at the master's factory!"

"My! How glad I am!" exclaimed Paula.

"Yes, Mademoiselle, but I have you to thank for your great kindness to me."

"I," said Paula in surprise; "why what have I done?"

"You, Mademoiselle! You made me feel that you really loved me. Also, you persuaded me that God loved me, miserable sinner that I am. But if tonight in this district you find one more honorable man and one criminal less, let us first thank God, and then you, Mademoiselle!"

"Do you own a New Testament?" said Paula as the Breton started to leave.

"A New Testament; what's that?"

"It's a book—a part of the Bible—that tells us about the Lord Jesus, and how He saves us from the guilt and power of sin, and how we can serve Him."

"Well, Mademoiselle," replied the Breton, "if it's a book, it's of no use to me. I don't know how to read!"

Paula looked at him with a mixture of surprise and pity.

"I might have been able to read," continued the poor fellow. "My mother sent me to school, but I scarcely ever actually appeared in the school-room. The streets in those days were too attractive a playground."

"But you could begin to learn even now!"

"No, Mademoiselle," and the Breton shook his head sadly, "It's too late now to get anything of that sort in this dull head."

Paula said nothing more at the time, but I could see that she had something in her mind relative to this new problem.

Chapter Four

THE YOUNG SCHOOL-MISTRESS

The following day Paula had a word with my father regarding the matter.

"Now don't worry any more about the Breton, Paula," he answered. "He knows enough to do what's necessary to gain his living, and if he wants to work faithfully and not spend all his money on drink, he can do that without knowing how to read. However, if it bothers you because he cannot read, why don't you advise him to go to night-school? I can't imagine what could have happened to him, but he's changed mightily, and for the better. I only hope the change in him will last!"

* * * * *

The days grew longer, the snow disappeared and the trees and fields began to put on their spring clothes. Week by week the Breton's home also began to show a marvelous transformation. The pigs who formerly found the garden a sort of happy rooting-ground now found themselves confronted with a neat fence that resisted all their attacks, and the garden itself with its well-raked beds, showed substantial promise of a harvest of onions, potatoes and cabbage in the near future. Spotless white curtains and shiny panes of window-glass began to show in place of the dirty rags and paper which used to stop part of the winter winds from entering, and the rain which formerly kept merry company with the wind in that unhappy dwelling now found itself completely shut out by shingles on the roof and sidewalls; and a certain air of neatness and order so pervaded the whole place that it became the talk of the little town.

"That's all very well, but it's not going to last long," said some.

161

"Well, we shall soon see," said others.

The Breton had to stand a good many jests and taunts from his former companions but he took it all without either complaint or abatement of his courage.

"I don't blame you one bit," he said to one of his tormentors, "for I was once exactly the same,—only I hope some day you'll be different too. In the meantime, comrade, I'll be praying for you."

"You must admit I'm a changed man, anyway," he said one day to a group who made sport of him.

"That's true, right enough," said one of them.

"Well, who changed me?"

Various opinions were offered to this question.

"Well, I'll tell you!" he thundered, and that stentorian voice which always used to dominate every assembly in which he mingled, held them spellbound!

"It was the Lord Jesus Christ. He died for me—yes, and He died for every one of you. He shed His blood on Calvary's cross to keep every man from hell who surrenders to Him in true repentance. Then He does another thing! His Holy Spirit takes away the bad habits of every man who surrenders to Him. He said once, 'If the Son shall make you free, ye shall be free indeed!' Now you look well at me! You know what a terrible temper I had. You've tried your best in these past weeks to make me angry but you haven't succeeded. That's a miracle in itself. You can say what you like to me now but you won't make me lose my temper. That's not to my credit, let me tell you! It's God Himself who's done something that I don't yet clearly understand. The money I earn, I dump it all in my wife's lap, for I know she can handle it better than I can! Then there's another thing! When I get up in the morning now, I ask God to help, and He does it. When I go to bed at night, I pray again. Let me tell you, if I should die, I'll go to heaven, and there I'll meet my dear old mother, for it's not what I've done, it's what *He's* done! It isn't that I'm any better than any of you. No! There isn't one of you as bad as I was," he continued, "but if God was able to change and pardon a beast like me, He can surely do the same with all of you. So what I say is, why don't you all do just the same as I've done? Surrender yourselves into the Christ's hands!"

Little by little, seeing it was useless to try to bring the Breton back into his old ways, his tormentors were silenced at last, and a life of new activities commenced for the former drunkard.

"You certainly appear to be quite happy," said Paula, as we passed the Breton's garden one evening where he was whistling merrily at his work.

"I certainly am that," said he, raising his head. "There's just one weight on my heart yet, however."

"And what's that?" Paula's voice was sympathetic.

"It's that I cannot read."

"But I didn't think that that fact interested you very much."

"Yes, I know, Mademoiselle, but I didn't comprehend what I had lost, but now I'd give my left hand if I could only read."

"Poor Breton," I said. It seemed to me we were a bit helpless before such a problem.

"It isn't that I want to become a fine gentleman, and all that;" and the Breton turned to address me also—"It's simply that I want to be able to read the Great Book that tells about God and His Son Jesus Christ. Also I would like to help my children that they might have a better chance than hitherto I have given them. But there you are! I'm just a poor ignorant man, and I suppose I always shall be."

"Well," said Paula, "why don't you attend the night school?"

"No, Mademoiselle," and the Breton shook his head; "that's all very well for the young fellows who have learned a little something and wish to learn a bit more. But me! At my age! I don't even know the letter A from the letter B, and I have such a dull head that I would soon tire out the best of teachers."

"Well, supposing I tried teaching you?" said Paula timidly.

"You, Mademoiselle!" cried the Breton stupefied, "you to try such a thing as to teach me!"

"And why not, if my uncle should let me?"

"Well, Mademoiselle, that would be different. I believe that with you to teach me I might be able to learn," and the Breton leaned on his spade for a moment.

"You are so good and kind and patient. I would not be afraid of your making fun of my stupid efforts. But there, there's no use thinking about such a thing, for I'm sure the master would never permit it."

*   *   *   *   *

In fact, it did take a good deal to persuade my father, but Paula won his permission at last.

The Breton came every Saturday night. Teresa complained a bit at first, seeing her kitchen turned into a night-school for such a rough ignorant workman, but "for Jesus Christ's sake," as Paula said, she had finally become resigned to it.

It was both pathetic and comical to see the efforts which the poor Breton made as he tried to follow with one great finger the letters which his young teacher pointed out to him. He stumbled on, making many mistakes but never discouraged. Sometimes the sweat poured from him when the task appeared too great for him. At such times he would put his head in his hands for a moment, and then with a great sigh he would start again.

"Oh, let him go!" said Teresa; "He's like myself. He'll never, never learn."

But Paula's eyes opened wide.

"Why! I simply can't abandon him unless he should give it up himself. Besides, have you forgotten, Teresa, what it cost me to learn to sew? But in the end I *did* learn; didn't I?"

So Teresa was silenced. But once the Breton had conquered his first barrier to learning his progress was truly surprising. In the factory his "primer" was always with him. At lunch hours he would either study alone, or he'd persuade a fellow-worker more advanced than himself to help with his lesson. Paula was astonished to see how quickly she could teach him a verse in the New Testament or a Waldensian hymn she had learned in the valley back home.

Nevertheless a week or two later she noticed that he seemed to be a bit distraught, and she feared he was getting weary of his task.

"What's the matter?" she finally asked him.

"Oh, nothing," and the Breton grinned rather sheepishly.

"Tell me, Breton, what's on your mind?"

He "guffawed" loudly as he replied. "You'd make fun of me sure, if I told you—and with good reason!"

"I never make fun of anybody," said Paula reproachfully.

"No, Mademoiselle, I ought to know that better than anybody else! Well, perhaps it might be well to tell you. If you must know it, it's this. There are many, I find, that wish they could be in my place tonight."

"In your place tonight! I'm afraid I don't understand," said Paula.

"Well, you see, I've got four or five of my old comrades who also want to learn to read."

"What's that you say?" Teresa said, leaving her knitting to stand in front of the Breton.

"It's true enough, Mademoiselle Teresa, and when you come to think of it, it's not a bit strange. Down at the factory they all know how different and how happy I am. And how they did make fun of me when I started to learn to read; just as they jeered at me when Jesus Christ first saved me and I learned to pray. But now some of them, seeing how happy I am, also want to learn to read, and who knows but some day they will want to know how to pray to the Lord Jesus also."

Paula's face took on a serious expression—finally, however, she slowly shook her head.

"You know, with all my heart, I'd just love to see it done; but it's perfectly useless, I suppose, even to think of it," she said sadly.

"That's what I thought too," said the Breton; "I'm sorry I spoke about it."

"Well, I don't know," continued Paula. "Perhaps if uncle could arrange somehow—I remember when I was quite small, back there before I left the valley, my dear godmother had a night-school for laboring men. It was just lovely. They learned to read and to write and to calculate. Then afterwards, each night before they went home they would sing hymns and read the Bible and pray."

"Yes, that's all very well," said Teresa, "but your godmother was a whole lot older than you are."

Then turning to Breton she said, "Why don't you tell your friends to go to the night-school in town?"

"Well," said the Breton, "I know that they learn many things there, but they don't teach them about God. However, as I said before, I'm sorry I mentioned the thing. Let's not speak any more about it."

"Well," said Paula, " I know what I'm going to do. I'll speak to the Lord Jesus about it."

And Paula kept her promise.

One morning, Teresa usually not at all inquisitive, could not seem to keep her eyes off a certain little group who were engaged in moving out of one of the "Red Cottages" across the road. More than once she paused in her work of tidying up the house to peer out of one window or another.

"That's the very best of all the 'Red Cottages,' and they're moving out of it," remarked Teresa finally.

"Of what importance is that?" I said to her rather sharply. I was washing windows, and that task always made me irritable.

"I've got a certain idea!" Teresa said.

"Tell me your big idea," I said.

"No! You go ahead and wash your windows. I'll tell you tomorrow."

The next day I had forgotten Teresa and her "idea." As I started for school she called after me, "Tell Mademoiselle Virtud, your teacher, that I want to see her just as soon as possible. I have to speak to her about something."

In flash I remembered what had happened the day before, and I guessed at once her secret.

"Teresa!" I cried, "I've got it now! You want Mademoiselle Virtud to occupy the house across the road. Oh, that'll be just wonderful!"

Teresa tried to put on her most severe air, but failed completely.

"Well, supposing that's not so!" she said, as with a grin she pushed me out of the door.

Mademoiselle Virtud came over that very afternoon. I hadn't been mistaken. She and Teresa went immediately across the road to see the empty house, the owner having left the key with us. At the end of a half-hour they returned.

"It's all arranged," and Teresa beamed. "She's coming to live here right across the road. I've thought of the thing for a long time, and now at last the house I wanted is empty.

Monsieur Bouche has promised to fix the fence and put a new coat of paint on the house, and with some of our plants placed in the front garden, it will be a fitting place for your dear teacher and her Gabriel to live in."

"You'll certainly spoil us!" said Mlle. Virtud. "What a joy it will be to leave that stuffy apartment in town. And Gabriel is so pale and weak! This lovely air of the open country will make a new boy of him!"

It was a wonderful time we had, arranging things before our new neighbors moved in. Teresa bought some neat linen curtains for the windows of the little house. Paula and I gathered quantities of flowers from our garden and placed them over the chimney-piece, and on the bedroom shelves and in the window-seats—and how the floors and windows did shine after we had finished polishing them!

When our teacher arrived in a coach with Gabriel packed in among the usual quantity of small household things of all kinds, great was her gratitude and surprise to find, in the transformed house, such signs of our care and affection for her. It was indeed the happiest moving day that could possibly be imagined. There wasn't a great quantity of furniture, and in an hour or so after our new neighbors' arrival we had everything installed in its proper place, to say nothing of the bright fire burning in the tiny grate and the kettle singing merrily above it. One would hardly have dreamed that it had been an empty house that very morning. Even Louis who had come home for a weekend holiday had sailed in and worked with us in putting the little cottage in order.

That night the newly-arrived tenants ate with us, after which Louis carried Gabriel pick-a-back to his new home across the road.

Our teacher's prophecy regarding Gabriel was a correct one. Day by day he grew stronger. Teresa looked out for him during school-hours, and with his bright happy ways he soon became a great favorite with the neighborhood boys.

*   *   *   *   *

"Tell me, Paula," said my father one evening, "how is the new pupil coming on?"

"Which new pupil?" our cousin said as she came and stood by my father's chair, where he sat reading his paper.

"The Breton, of course. Surely you haven't more than one pupil?"

"For the present, no!" she answered, with a queer little smile on her quiet face.

"For the present, no." repeated my father; "and what may that mean?"

Paula rested her cheek against the top of my father's head.

"Dearest uncle," she said, "will you please grant me a great favor?"

"Now, what?" said my father—and the stern, serious face lighted up with a smile.

"You see, the Breton has almost learned to read, and it would be just splendid if some of his old comrades and his two sons could learn, too."

"Oh, Paula, Paula!" said my father—"where is all this going to end?"

But Paula was not easily daunted, especially when the thing asked for was for the benefit of other people.

"Now, why won't you let me teach them, dear uncle?" She came and kneeled at my father's feet, and took both his hands in hers.

"But you're only a very young and very little student, Paula. You must be taught yourself before you can teach others." My father's voice was very tender, but firm as well, and it didn't look to me as if Paula would win. She said nothing in reply, but stayed kneeling there at his feet with those great appealing eyes of hers fixed on his face.

"We shall see, we shall see," said my father gently, "when you've finished your own studies. Besides I think you're reasonable enough to see that such a task along with your studies would be too big a burden for a child like you. I could not let you take this up."

"I suppose you're right, dear uncle," said Paula humbly, as she rose and rested her head against my father's shoulder, "and yet if you could only know how happy it would make the Breton and his comrades. And besides," she added, "I had fondly hoped that if I could have taught them, they would learn much about the Lord Jesus and take Him as their Saviour, as the Breton has done."

"You seem to think of nothing but how to serve your 'Lord Jesus,'" and there was a wistful sort of tone in my father's voice.

"Well, am I not His servant?"

"No!" said my father, "I'd call you a soldier of His, and one that's always under arms!"

"That's because I have such a wonderful, such a kind and such a powerful Captain. I wish everybody might come to know Him! And to know Him is to love Him!"

There followed a moment of silence, so solemn, so sweet that it seemed as if a Presence had suddenly entered, and I personally felt my soul in that moment suddenly lifted toward God as it had never been before. And as I looked at Paula standing so humbly there her eyes seemed to say: "Oh, my uncle, my cousin, would that you, too, might love Him and receive Him as the Saviour of your soul!"

"Listen, Paula," my father said; "will you leave the Breton and his friends and his sons in my hands for the present?"

Paula looked at him searchingly for a moment, as if trying to find out what was in his mind.

"Of course!" she finally said.

"Well, then, just rest content. I'll try to see the thing through somehow. If I'm not very much mistaken, these protégés of yours will have very little to complain of."

"Oh, uncle dear!" shouted Paula in delight, "what are you planning to do?"

"I don't know yet exactly, but I've thought of something. No! No! Don't try to thank me for anything, for I don't know how it will come out. But," he smiled as he laid his hand on Paula's head, "you certainly have a method of asking for things I don't seem to find any way to refuse you."

Chapter Five

THE NIGHT SCHOOL

For the first time in my life a great secret had been confided
to me. Of course, I felt quite proud that they had considered
me important enough to be a sharer of the secret. But my!
What a struggle it was not to tell Paula!

In a few days it would be Paula's fifteenth birthday, and the
whole family seemed endued with the same idea, to make it an
especially happy and unforgettable occasion.

Paula must have suspected something with all the coming
and going; the whispering and smothered giggles in the
corners, etc., but she wasn't the kind to pry into other people's
affairs, and so, no matter what she may have thought, she kept
her own counsel.

On the morning of the great day, which to our great
satisfaction, came on a Sunday, Paula was quite surprised to
find that Mlle. Virtud and Gabriel had been invited over to
breakfast; but aside from that occurrence there was nothing
unusual yet to indicate that we were celebrating Paula's
birthday.

When the meal was finished, however, my father folded up
his napkin, and with an air of mock gravity said, "Why, let me
see, this is Paula's birthday, isn't it? I suppose Paula's been
wondering why there were no gifts piled up on her plate. You
see, Paula, we've all combined on the one gift, but it's too big
to put on the dinner table. However, it's not far away. Let's
all go and have a look together."

He led the way out of the house across the road, and we all
followed.

I presume the neighborhood received quite a shock of
surprise to see such a procession of folks coming out of the big

172

house. Many came and stood in their front door-yards to view the unusual sight, for instance, of Louis with his arm linked in that of our old servant Teresa, and Paula herself on our father's arm, and the rest of us strung out behind.

We finally stopped in front of Mlle. Virtud's newly painted little house, with its tiny garden in front in all the splendor of spring dress.

"Come in, Paula," said our teacher of former days. "Your present is in here in this front room."

We all followed after Paula, eager to see the result of her inspection of the "present."

Paula took one step, and then stopped on the threshold.

"What do you think of your birthday present, Paula?" said my father. "Do you think the Breton and his comrades will be content to come here to study and to learn to sing, etc., in this room?"

"Oh, uncle dear!" and that was all she could say as she embraced and kissed him with a gratitude we all knew well was too deep for mere words to express.

Suddenly Louis pulled her hair a bit, saying, "Well, how about the rest of us. Aren't you going to thank us too? There are a lot of folks here that have had a share in this business."

Paula gave him a smile in which she included all of us in her thankful joy and gratitude.

"Why!" said Paula, "this is the room everybody thought was useless, and which was in such bad condition that the landlord didn't think it worthwhile to fix up!"

"Yes," said my father; "it's the very room. I confess one would hardly recognize it, but when Monsieur Bouche understood what it was to be used for, he went to unusual trouble to fix it properly. You'll have to thank him especially, Paula. He has a reputation of being not always so amiable."

"I will take him a lovely bunch of flowers," said Paula.

"Humph!" said Louis, "I'm sure I don't know what he'd do with them. He doesn't often get flowers from his tenants."

Paula walked about the room as in a dream, examining everything.

The table in the center had been loaned by Dr. Lebon. The lovely red curtains were a present from Mlle. Virtud. Rosa and Louis had given the two long benches on each side of the table. My father had given the school-books, and I had bought the pencils and copy-books from my monthly allowance. It was all very simple and severe, but to Paula's eyes these gifts brought together in the little white-washed room seemed to her quite wonderful.

"Look up there," said Louis, "you haven't seen that yet," and Paula saw hanging from the ceiling a fine new lamp to which a white paper seemed to be tied. Louis reached up and took down the paper for her, and she read as follows: "In great gratitude from the Breton."

"Now, look here," said Louis, "you don't need to weep over it! The Breton is only grateful for all you've done for him. Thanks to you, he's been able to save up a little money lately instead of spending it all on drink."

"Now, look here," said Louis, "you don't need to weep to an elaborately embroidered motto on the wall containing the Lord's words to the weary ones of earth. 'Come unto Me, all ye that labor and are heavy laden, and I will give you rest.'"

"Oh, it's all too much!" said Paula completely overcome. "How can I thank you all for what you've done?"

"Your gratitude and happiness is sufficient reward for us," said my father. "I don't know what put the idea in our heads. I suppose you will say it was God, and perhaps you are right. All I know is that I spoke to Mlle. Virtud of your desire to have a night-school for the Breton and his friends, and then spoke to others about it and—well, now you've seen the result.

You owe most of your thanks to Mlle. Virtud who brought the thing about and gave us the use of the room."

"Which room," said Mlle. Virtud, with a dry little smile, "had no value whatsoever, you'll remember."

"And another thing," said my father, "she is the one who has taken over the responsibility of the night-school. Otherwise I could not have permitted you to take up such a task. Then Rosa is going to help when she can, and Lisita has an idea she can do something also."

"And I," said Louis, "where do I come into the picture?"

With a grin my father turned to his son, "That's where you're only in the background for once."

It was decided, in accord with Mlle. Virtud, to have classes twice a week. Thursdays would be for reading, writing and arithmetic, and Sundays would be a time for learning songs and for putting their studies into practice by reading in the Bible, and, for what several had been asking, namely, to learn how to pray.

If the Breton was a model scholar, this could not be said of his two younger sons. These boys appeared to be much below the average in natural intelligence, besides the fact that their ordinary educational opportunities had, as in the case of Joseph, their older brother, been decidedly neglected. Their father had compelled them to attend the "night-school," but apparently they didn't seem to grasp what it was all about. Without any apparent cause they both would suddenly duck down below the table to hide their merriment. Whatever story, no matter how interesting, was read aloud, they didn't appear to comprehend a word of it, and if a chapter from the Bible was read they either showed elaborate signs of boredom or else they would doze in their seats. Paula would gaze at them sadly—her heart was grieved at such colossal indifference.

The three comrades of the Breton, however, were decidedly different, taking up their studies with great eagerness and listening well to everything that was read aloud.

"It's a whole lot better here than spending our money at the liquor shop," they would say with a smile of satisfaction.

"I'll say so," the Breton would chime in. "I'll tell you what, comrades, if I'd known only before all that one gains in Christ's service, I would have started long ago on this new life with Him."

The happiest and most beloved of all in the school was Gabriel. He was so happy that he was able to come in and study with the others; and when it came to singing, his marvelously fresh and clear tones outclassed them all—that is, all but one.

I seem to hear yet those lovely hymns that were sung with such sincerity and heartiness.

Chapter Six

THE HOUSE OF GOD

It was vacation time—in August. Teresa said she had never seen a dryer or a hotter summer in her whole existence. Gabriel and his sister had gone to visit their family in the country and we had our usual "red letter" time at Grandmother Dumas' house. We had returned from our visit greatly refreshed—all except Paula, who seemed to have lost somewhat of that perpetual happiness which, when she appeared on the scene had always been such a tonic to us all. She had tried her best not to show it, but she gave us all the impression that she tired very quickly.

"I think the reason you tire so soon is because you're growing so quickly," said Teresa. Paula laughed and said that that wasn't her fault.

One morning my father seemed to be looking at her more intently than usual. He finally said, "You're not feeling well; are you, Paula?"

"I'm all right, dear uncle," she said. "Sometimes I get a bit tired. I think it must be the heat."

"But, my dear child, you hardly eat anything at all, and you've lost those roses in your cheeks."

He still continued looking at her,—then suddenly he said, "I'll tell you one thing that I think would please you very much. Do you know what that would be?"

"What, sir?" and Paula seemed to regain all her usual animation.

"I think," said my father slowly in a low voice as if talking to himself, "I think you"—and he paused a moment—"What would you say if you were to go to church with Celestina on Sunday?"

177

"Oh, dear uncle, could I really go?" Paula jumped to her feet excitedly.

"Yes, I think I'll let you go—and"—again he hesitated a bit—"if Teresa, Rosa and Lisita wish to, they may go along too."

"And you, dear uncle, will you not come with us?" questioned Paula, as she looked into the sad, stern face that had softened considerably of late.

"We shall see, we shall see. But you'd better not count on me. My, oh, me! Just see! Those roses have all come back again!"

"Well, but you don't know how happy you've made me!" said Paula as she fairly danced out of the house with me to tell the news to Celestina.

"Well," said Celestina, "all I can say is that the Lord heard my prayers and yours, dear Paula. It's the great weapon of the weak and needy, and in fact can be the power to serve all and anyone who will surrender themselves and all they are into the hands of the Saviour."

We had seated ourselves near the door of her little cottage. Something in the deep tones of the old lady's voice seemed to search my very heart. We always enjoyed listening to this old saint who, like Enoch and Noah, walked with God. We seemed to be drawn closer to God in her humble little cottage than in any other place.

"You see," she continued, "I'm old and quite feeble, and besides I'm poor, and can't do very much for folks; but there's one thing I can do, and that is, pray. And I do pray for everybody—and especially for you and your family, my dear friends. God doesn't let me see many results of my prayers, but that doesn't discourage me. I just keep everlastingly at it, and I can leave the results to Him. Has He not said, through the mouth of His Apostle John, 'This is the confidence that we have in Him, that if we ask anything according to His will, He heareth us, and if we know that He hear us, whatsoever we ask, we know that we have the petitions that we desired of Him.'

"I remember once hearing a certain hymn about prayer. I never could remember all the verses, but most of it has remained deeply engraved in my memory although I only heard it once. It was sung by a young missionary from Africa who happened to be passing through Paris. It was at a meeting which I attended as a young girl many years ago."

"Please sing it to us, dear Celestina," said Paula, "even though you may not remember it all."

"Well, my dear young friends," said Celestina, "that old hymn has been my comfort and the inspiration of my prayers though all the years since I heard it sung so long ago in Paris where I lived when I was young. Here it is:" and as those quavering notes sounded we seemed lifted toward the heavenly Throne of which she sang.

On heavenly heights an Angel stands.
He takes our prayer in heavenly hands,
And with celestial incense rare,
He mingles every heart-felt prayer
Of those who trust His precious blood
To reconcile their souls to God.

Then from that glorious heavenly place
Descend the lightnings of His grace;
To heal, to strengthen and provide
For those who trust in Him who died.
"Who died," I say? — Yea, He who rose
Triumphant, Conqueror of His foes!

Who is this priestly Angel bright

Who thus dispels our darkest night?
'Tis He who sets the captive free,
Jesus who died on Calvary's tree;

Who is, who was, and is to come—
The glory of His Father's Home!

"Well," said Paula softly as the last note died away, "I've
prayed much for my dear uncle that he might be saved."

"And God will hear and answer you, my dear, according to
the scripture I've just quoted. Let me tell you something.
Your uncle came here to see me a few days ago, and I believe
he is not far from the kingdom of God!"

"Oh," cried Paula, "I would give everything to see him truly
saved!"

*   *   *   *   *

Never had I seen Paula so happy as when we entered the
little evangelical church in the Rue San Eloi.

We had had the natural timidity of new-comers, and had
feared more than anything else that battery of eyes which
would surely be turned on us at our entrance. It was therefore
a great relief to find that the meeting had already begun, and
an empty pew well toward the back that held us all, seemed to
beckon to us with a sort of mute welcome.

Hardly were we seated when I noticed Paula (who had of
course been accustomed to church-going at her old home in
the valley) had kneeled, and with her eyes closed seemed to be
offering a prayer. This was soon ended and she resumed her
seat. It was all so new to me that I could not at first take in
much of the details of the service.

The preacher had a fine noble face which seemed to me that
a quiet smile of approval passed over his face as his eyes

rested on Paula who so fervently joined in the songs—all of which seemed quite familiar to her.

It was an affecting thing, that vision of my girl companion. In her white dress with its blue sash at the waist, and with her wide white straw hat, she made a lovely picture. In that frank open countenance I think I read her thoughts. Here in God's house she had entered once more the Promised Land from which she had been exiled for four long years!

Suddenly the sun came from behind a cloud, especially designed, I thought, to send a ray of rose-colored light through one of the stained-glass windows of the church over that beautiful face at my side which now showed only rapt attention to the simple gospel message saturated with God's Word that flowed like a mighty river from the preacher's lips.

As we came through the door on our way out, I caught a glimpse of my father's tall form just disappearing around a bend in the Rue San Eloi. I think he must have stolen up to the door and had been listening outside!

Chapter Seven

IN HIS PRESENCE

At times I have wished to efface from my mind the memory of those last moments that Paula was with us. Yet as I think of the House of Glory to which she will go, and also the manner in which she went (in the path of duty as a good soldier of the Cross) I bless God and kneel in gratitude to Him for having loaned her to bring us all to the bleeding side of the Saviour, and thus make us new creatures in Christ Jesus.

*　　*　　*　　*　　*

It was on the Wednesday after that Sunday when we had first attended church. It had been a day of terrible heat. The oppressive atmosphere seemed to promise an electric storm. Louis who had forgotten a study book when he went to school on Monday, had returned to get it. Paula had tried to study, but I could see she was having great difficulty.

Suddenly Teresa appeared and called Paula to take a letter which my father wished to send to a man who lived in the Rue Fourmi.

"Go quickly, Paula, there's a storm brewing, but I think you can easily get back before it breaks. The Rue Fourmi is not far away."

Paula had no time to answer before Teresa disappeared again to the other end of the house.

Paula turned to Louis, who was about to start out for his uncle's house, where he stayed during the week in order to be near his school.

"Louis dear," she said, "won't you please take this letter on your way back to your uncle's house?"

"No," said Louis sharply; "I never go that way."

"No, I know that; but it would only be a few steps out of your way to leave it there, and—well—you see—I have quite a headache."

"Teresa told you to take the letter, not me. A fig for your headache! It's only that you're too lazy to stir!" said Louis.

"Louis!" I shouted, "You ought to be ashamed of yourself! You know well enough Paula's always willing to do anything for anybody! I'd go myself, but I simply can't leave what I'm doing now. If Teresa had remembered, she would have given you the letter and you know it! If you don't take it, I'll tell father!"

"Do as you please," said Louis coolly. "I'll not be bothered with it!"

I was furious and couldn't keep back angry tears that now began to roll down my cheeks.

"Never mind, Lisita," said Paula, as she ran for her hat. Then as she went through the door she turned for a last look at Louis, "Won't you please take it, Louis?" she said.

"No!" said Louis—"and that's that!" and he turned his back to Paula.

"Good-bye, Louis dear!" she finally said without the least show of anger, as she left the house. "We'll be seeing you again on Saturday."

She ran down the street quickly in order to return before the gathering storm broke.

Louis followed shortly to return to his uncle's, whistling cheerfully as he went; but his cheerfulness seemed to me to be a little too exaggerated to be real.

After I'd finished my task I sought out Teresa at the other end of the great house.

"Paula has a bad headache," I said.

"Why didn't she tell me that?" said Teresa. "I'd have sent Louis, but I didn't think of it at the time."

I opened my mouth to say something, and then I shut it again. I had begun slowly to learn from Paula's example not to be a "tattle-tale."

Meanwhile the sky grew darker. Suddenly Teresa said, "I don't know what's keeping Paula. Here, Lisita! Take this umbrella and go and meet her. I'm afraid she'll be caught in the rain before she gets back."

I soon found her as she turned in at the bottom of Rue Darnetal. "We must hurry," she said as the thunder began to mutter in the distance. Hardly had she spoken when a flash of lightening almost blinded us. This was followed almost immediately by a great crash of thunder that seemed to shake the very ground beneath our feet. Then came a sound of confused shouts as if something had happened at the other end of a cross street that we were passing. Could it be a house had been struck by the lightening? No, the shouts increased and changed to cries of terror. Soon we guessed the cause, as we heard a rushing sound of galloping horses, which, frightened by the flash and the clap of thunder, came in sight around a bend in the street enveloped in a cloud of dust, dragging a heavy wagon behind them. Instinctively Paula retreated to a protecting doorway and I huddled in terror close beside her.

"Lisita!" she called suddenly. "Look! Look!"

What I saw seemed to freeze my blood! Directly in the pathway of the onrushing horses, totally unconscious of his danger, was a little boy of about three years old toddling along in the middle of the road. One instant more and it would have been all over! Suddenly Paula left our shelter like a shot from a gun. Then I heard a sharp cry that rent the air like a knife, and then—I can remember little more—just a confusion of people running hither and thither, and then for me all was darkness, but in that darkness I seemed to hear still that piercing cry of anguish.

*   *   *   *   *

When I came back to consciousness I found myself in the sofa in our dining-room, with Catalina bathing my face and hands with cold water.

"Where's Paula?" I cried, for I remembered at once that terrible scene in the Rue Darnetal.

"Paula is in her room," said Catalina, turning her head to hide the tears that would come in spite of all her efforts.

I tried to rise and go to our room.

"Stay where you are, Lisita!" said Catalina. "You may go a bit later when you're feeling stronger."

But now a terrible suspicion crossed my mind. "Catalina," I cried, almost beside myself with fear, "Tell me the truth! Is Paula dead?"

"No, Lisita; Paula's not dead," as she tried in vain to detain me; "She is still breathing—and"—but I heard nothing more. My legs trembled strangely as I stumbled toward our bedroom. Once there, again that terrible darkness started to come over me, but it was only a momentary weakness. With an effort I steadied myself as I came near the bed where my dearest one lay so still—that lovely face so white, the lips slightly parted with just a faint stirring of the breath.

The room was full of people, some weeping silently, some trying to choke back their sobs. Others, like my father and Dr. Lebon, with an agony showing on their faces much more terrible than any tears.

All this I saw as in a horrible dream from which I hoped to awake at any moment. But no!—I soon realized it was all too true. This was the first real grief of my life, and I had to sustain it alone for I had not yet yielded to Him who sends comfort to His children in their time of anguish. He did take pity on me, however. In the next room I hid my grief in

Teresa's arms—Teresa, who more than anyone else, knew the
love that had united me to Paula.

"Oh, Teresa," I cried when I found myself alone with her;
"she must not die! She must not! I simply cannot live without
her, you know that! Oh, pray for *me*, dear Teresa. God will
hear your prayer. He probably wouldn't hear mine. Tell Him!
Oh, please tell Him, Paula must not die!"

"No, Lisita," Teresa said as she dried my tears; "We must
leave Paula in God's hands. He loves her more than you and I
could ever do. If you could see that poor broken body as I've
see it you would not ask that she should live! Yes, indeed, she
was happy with us.   She was to us all like an angelic
messenger sent from God to draw us to Him and to show us
the way to heaven.   And now He's called her to Himself
almost without suffering, for she appears to have become
insensible from the instant that the horse struck her down.
Listen to me, Lisita! Soon Paula will be at her Saviour's side,
her Saviour whom she loved so well.

"We must think of her happiness, dear Lisita, not our own,
from this day forward. Paula, you remember, never thought of
herself. Her thought was always for others, and it was for
another that she died. She gave her life to save that little boy.
So she followed in the footsteps of her Saviour, as a good
soldier of the Lord Jesus who died to save all who repent and
believe on His blessed name."

The voice of our old servant, so tender, so motherly, seemed
to heal my sorrow. When I became calmer she told me some
of the details of the tragedy. Paula had dashed in front of the
horses just in time to throw the child out of danger but had
been unable to escape herself. That much I understood; but
from that day to this, I have never been able to bring myself to
ask for any more details. It seems I had fainted, and they
carried us both home.

Poor Teresa, I knew how ardently she, too, loved our Paula, but courageous and unselfish her only thought, as ever, was for us. In consoling me she forgot her own sorrow. As I looked at that strong calm face lighted up as from an inner brilliance, it seemed to take on a striking likeness to the dear one whose life was ebbing away in the next room. There came to my mind a verse from a Bible story that Paula had told us once. It was this:

"The spirit of Elijah hath fallen on Elisha."

*   *   *   *   *

A stream of neighbors came in from everywhere. It was in those last moments as these humble friends passed before that unconscious form that we came to comprehend how many lives had been touched by the simple country girl from the Waldensian mountains. Some remembered her just from the smile with which she always greeted young and old as she passed up and down the long street at our end of the town. Others spoke of the loving adoration of the children whom she had protected and defended. Still others mentioned the kindness she had shown them, and poured out many stories of Paula's universal love for all—of her visits to the poor and sick, and of how she had pointed them to the Saviour who had died to take away their sin; bringing joy and hope and liberty into many a home where only discord and misery had reigned before.

So the tears of many of our humble, friendless neighbors mingled with our own as we waited for the end.

But there was one on whom the blow fell more terribly than on any one of the rest of us, for it was a bitter mixture of remorse and shame that Louis had to bear. When he arrived at the house after being summoned from our uncle's place, and came to a full realization of what had happened, for an instant he seemed to turn to stone. Then a sharp cry came from him.

In that short moment he seemed to change from a careless, selfish boy to a man—a man awakened at last to his terrible need of a change and with a transforming purpose in his life from that day forward.

Louis demanded that I tell everybody present what had happened that afternoon. When I refused, he poured out the whole sorry, sordid story of his selfishness without one word of excuse, saying as he finished, "So you see, it was I who killed her, for there was no need of her stirring from the house." Then he turned to my father imploring him to punish him severely. He said he could ask no pardon, for he had done what he considered unpardonable. For answer my father took him in his arms; and I knew that at that moment my father and Louis came to understand each other better than they had ever done in their lives before.

"No, my poor boy," my father said; "you need no further punishment. Now go to your heavenly Father and ask Him to make you His child." And I know that Louis did so.

*   *   *   *   *

In silence we waited. Paula was the bond of love that had united us all; not only to one another but now also to God. How wonderful, how beautiful, had been that short life, and how she had poured out her love upon us. Again the scene came back to me of the moonlight night at this same bedside, when at prayer she had seemed more like an angel talking with the One who had sent her to us, than merely the simple, honest-hearted country girl that she really was.

Suddenly the door opened slowly and a woman poorly dressed entered, leading a little boy of about three years old. When he saw us he stopped and turned to hide behind the folds of his mother's dress.

"Come in, come in," said Teresa kindly, as she led them both to the side of my dear one lying there so white and still.

"Oh, Carlito," exclaimed the poor woman turning to her little son as she dropped on her knees beside the bed. "How I wish you could understand! This it that lovely one who saved your life! She took your place under the horses' hoofs!" Then taking Paula's two hands in her own she said, "Oh, Mademoiselle, oh, that you might hear me! Would that I might do something in return for what you have done for my boy! Oh, is there nothing I can do?"

"Yes, my dear woman," said our old servant—and her eyes were streaming—"I'll tell you what you can do. Nothing would have pleased Paula better than to have known that you had taken the Lord Jesus as your Saviour. Also you may take this dear child and dedicate and train him for God's service in the days to come."

"That," said the poor woman, "I solemnly promise to do if you will show me how."

Thus it was that our Teresa had the joy of pointing her first soul to the Saviour.

Tenderly my father cut off two locks of that beautiful hair of our dear one, and as the woman went out he said, "Take this one and keep it always in remembrance of the rescuer of your little boy; and this other one," and he held out the second to her also, "keep it for him until he's old enough to understand."

Taking them from my father's hand she silently kissed them and placed them in the bosom of her dress as she and her little one glided through the door.

Louis had gone out on a special errand, and he soon returned, bringing with him from the factory the object of his search. The poor Breton, followed by his sons and all the other "scholars" of the night-school, started to enter the room and then stopped abashed at the threshold. At the invitation of my father however, one by one they all came to the bedside, pale and shaken with emotion.

"I'm glad you were able to get here before the end came," said my father. "Oh, if you could only know how she loved you all!"

The Breton suddenly broke down and cried like a child. When he could control himself he said, "It was but this very morning that I passed her on the street. She seemed just like a happy bird as she waved me 'good day,'—and now—now—to find her dying here!"

"May the dear Lord's will be done!" said Teresa.

The poor Breton had buried his face in his hands, but suddenly looking up, he said humbly,

"You're quite right, Mademoiselle Teresa—but, you see, Mademoiselle Paula was more to me than it seems she could mean to any of you. I was a drunkard and a robber—a monster of iniquity! I was despised and hated and feared by everybody, and for good reason. But there in Celestina's kitchen that day, Mademoiselle was not afraid to take these rough hands—these hands that had been so often stained with crime and violence in her own pure white ones to tell me she would help me! She it was who taught me to pray. She it was who prayed for me while I was in prison. I have seen men ground to pieces in the gears of a machine in the factory. I've looked on death in many terrible forms without shedding a tear—but this one! Oh, Mademoiselle Paula! Would that I could have died in your place!" And again quivering with emotion, the Breton turned and leaned against the wall to hide his tears.

Suddenly a convulsion shook the form of my dear one and Dr. Lebon stepped forward and took her hand. "The end is coming," he said.

My father dropped on his knees beside the bed. "Oh, Lord," he said, "I, too, would be Thine own. Is it too late for me?"

At that moment a hand was laid on his shoulder. It was the same hand that years ago had been laid on his wife's eyes to close them for the last time. That same hand had tended and cared faithfully for his children ever since.

"Monsieur! My good Master!" said Teresa, in a tone of tender love and respect such as I had never heard her use before, "It is not too late! He has said, 'Him that cometh unto Me, I will in no wise cast out.'"

My father looked up. "Well, then, Teresa,—I come to Him."

The dear old woman dropped on her knees and with folded hands simply said,

"Thanks, dear Lord, for Thou hast answered my prayer, and Paula's too!"

*   *   *   *   *

The storm of wind and rain had passed. In the little gardens of the "Red Cottages" across the street, the flowers once again began to raise their heads and the birds began to sing as the sun came out once more.

Suddenly there came a soft sigh from the still form on the bed. Dr. Lebon nodded as he turned away. His task was ended. The Good Shepherd had taken His tired lamb in His arms.

*   *   *   *   *

Then the sound of a deep voice was heard, saying,

"Except a corn of wheat fall into the ground and die it abideth alone, but if it die, it bringeth forth much fruit."

I recognized the voice at once—It was Celestina's.